2359

DATE DUE

FEB 2 1 2008			
JAN 2 0 2006			
DEC 07 2013			

2359

D0965252

TOM SWIFT®
THE RESCUE MISSION
VICTOR APPLETON

WANDERER BOOKS
Published by Simon & Schuster, New York

Published by WANDERER BOOKS
A Simon & Schuster Division of
Gulf & Western Corporation
Simon & Schuster Building
1230 Avenue of the Americas
New York, New York 10020

Manufactured in the United States of America
10 9 8 7 6 5 4 3 2 1
WANDERER and colophon are trademarks
of Simon & Schuster
TOM SWIFT is a trademark of Stratemeyer Syndicate,
registered in the United States Patent and Trademark Office

Library of Congress Cataloging in Publication Data
Appleton, Victor, pseud.
The rescue mission.
(Tom Swift ; #6)
Summary: Tom and his friends find themselves in
the hands of unfriendly robots who are trying to
eliminate all biological life from their planet.
[1. Science fiction. 2. Robots—Fiction]
I. Title.   II. Series: Appleton, Victor, pseud.
Tom Swift ; no. 6.
PZ7.A652Re 1982 [Fic] 81–19648
ISBN 0–671–43370–9   AACR2
ISBN 0–671–43386–5 (pbk.)

CONTENTS

Chapter One

Tom Swift's face was a picture of amazement. "What!" he gasped. "Are you *sure*?"

Aristotle, Tom's robot and favorite invention, nodded his metal head. "Yes, Tom, there can be no doubt about it. There is a special and, I might even say, mysterious transmission in the radio wavelength."

Tom twisted in the pilot's chair to face the impressive array of screens, buttons, and switches which lined his part of the spaceship's bridge. The *Exedra*, Tom's own starship, had provided the young inventor with many adventures. But he could not think of one which had begun quite so unexpectedly.

Benjamin Franklin Walking Eagle, Tom's co-pilot and best friend, was already checking the startling information Aristotle had described by running it through the *Exedra*'s main computer. Ben's face bore the same intense look of concentration that his Indian ancestors had worn while stalking buffalo so many generations before.

"Maybe it is some kind of static," Tom suggested.

"That's right," Anita Thorwald agreed. "After all, we are in deep space." The young redhead, the other member of the crew and a fast friend of both Tom and Ben, wrinkled her forehead in thought. "Out here there are all kinds of stars: pulsars, flare stars, infrared stars, and even X-ray stars. A lot of them would be broadcasting in this frequency range."

Tom grinned. "Remember when you were a little kid and thought that a star was just one of those twinkly white lights in the nighttime sky?" He shook his head in wonder.

Anita laughed. "And then you found out they were all different colors, not just the diamond-white they looked like from Earth."

"Yeah," Ben agreed. "And now there are all those different kinds. Sometimes I wish I could be a little kid again when all the stars did was twinkle and the most important thing I did was wish on them."

Tom laughed. "You don't really mean that, good buddy. If you were a little kid again, you'd have to give up your computers."

"Never!" Ben declared stoutly.

The young Indian's genius with computers and his knowledge of them had been what had drawn the two young men together in *Tom Swift: The City in the Stars*.

The screen in front of Ben suddenly flashed to life. "Aristotle's right!" he exclaimed. "There is something special about that signal!"

The mechanoid once again swiveled toward Tom. "There is no doubt about the matter. It is a manufactured transmission with discernible sequences."

"You mean there are *people* out here?" Anita asked incredulously.

"I did not say that, Anita," Aristotle replied quietly. "I only said that there were obvious sequences to the radio signal and that it was a manufactured—not accidental—transmission."

"Could be a lost space probe still sending out its signals," Ben pointed out, grinning impishly.

"Oh, please. Not one of *them* again!" Anita wailed in mock despair. In *Tom Swift: The Alien*

Probe, a mysterious mechanical messenger from outer space had provided quite a bit of excitement for the three friends and Aristotle.

"Aristotle, put the message on the TTU," Tom instructed, referring to one of his handiest inventions. The Teacher-Translator Unit instantly translated any language into the language of the wearer, enabling him or her to speak with a member of another culture without waiting the long time it would require to study a foreign language. Tom had installed a TTU in the *Exedra*'s main computer for use at just such times as this.

"I do not believe there is enough of a data base yet to adequately translate a message," the robot said. But he made the necessary connections.

A sizzle of static burst from a speaker.

"Sist Tak biological temmartralla isk intelligence quarla temro world glecca blorma pelzar biological flect toomarri—"

"What in the world is *that?*" Ben asked, astonished.

The partial translation continued. *"—teeka morro assistance fen yumar demma tulka genocide dorlanta quuturmara but beware Yulla justalma gulla tac!"*

"The message will repeat in twenty seconds," Aristotle informed them.

"It sounds like a cry for help," Anita said, brushing her hair out of her eyes.

"I think we should slow down the *Exedra* until we investigate this mysterious message a bit more," said Ben.

"Yes," Tom agreed, "it's hard to ignore someone asking for help."

"The TTU is getting more at each passage," Aristotle said. "It is a regrettably small data base."

The TTU semitranslated the next transmission and they heard the words "enslaved" and "annihilate." Then came the third transmission, and the four companions listened in fascination and with a growing sense of horror.

"To all sentient biological beings! Machine intelligence has enslaved Ourworld and seeks to annihilate all biological life forms. Ourworld desperately needs assistance to combat the threat of total genocide. Come at once but beware the Unimind!"

"Give me a hard copy on that, Ben," Tom said. He looked at his friends. "It's pretty clear, isn't it?"

Ben and Anita nodded gloomily. "What do we do now?" Ben asked.

Tom turned to Aristotle. "What do you think?"

"Tom, I am well aware of the prejudice many humans have against machine intelligence.

There are many lurid fictions in your literature where beings not unlike myself have taken over the world and enslaved humans."

"We know *you're* not like that," Anita said quickly.

"You can't be like that," Ben added. He was referring to elements of Aristotle's basic program which explicitly prevented him from ever harming a human being.

"Yes, but the myth still persists," the robot said. "Truly intelligent machine intelligence is something quite new to mankind, and I believe they view it as something even more alien than, say, the Skree."

The Skree were a race of aliens Tom and his friends had first contacted in *Tom Swift: The War in Outer Space*. Since then they had had another adventure with a member of the Skree race.

"Yes, but the message, Aristotle. What can you tell us about it?" Tom prompted.

"We have no idea how long this message has been transmitting. The transmitting station is not far off, only a few million miles to our stern, actually. But it could have been broadcasting automatically for centuries," the robot cautioned.

"In other words, it could be a dead issue not worth pursuing," Tom said.

"Yes, it could be. I have transmitted a signal back on the same wavelength, but so far there has been no response."

Tom turned to Ben and Anita. "Should we go check it out? Just look things over to see if this is something long gone?" He spread his hands in a questioning gesture.

"Well, if they are biological beings who are in distress, we have to go," said Ben. "No offense, Aristotle, but people are more important than machines."

"No offense taken, Ben," the robot replied. "I quite agree."

"You really want to go, don't you?" Anita said to Tom.

Tom grinned. "Well, I *am* curious," he admitted.

The redhead grinned back. "So am I!"

She gestured toward the stars which were shining in the bridge ports. "Everything we do out here in deep space is so new and exciting. I suppose there are probably lots of other space-traveling races who have done it all and are bored with space travel. But each new contact is a first for us and for the human race. Sure, let's go take a peek!"

"Just a peek," Ben cautioned.

Tom twisted around and settled into the pilot's couch. "Set the coordinates," he instructed Aristotle.

"It seems that every time we come into hyperspace to test some improvement in the stardrive we run into trouble," Anita said.

"What makes you think this is trouble?" Tom asked. "All we are doing is checking out a distress call."

"And the call might be centuries old," Ben added.

"I just have this feeling," Anita said softly. The young woman's abilities as an empath were well known by her two companions. They knew from past experience that Anita's extra ability to sense strong emotions was to be taken very seriously.

"But could your empathic abilities work across such vast distances?" Ben wondered.

"The whole area of empathic studies is too new," replied Anita. "There is much more to it than we know. Besides, we've never had the opportunity to conduct research in deep space, so who knows?"

"Anita is certainly right about one thing," Tom said quickly. "Until we know otherwise, we should treat this as a possibly dangerous mission. I'm going to program the *Exedra* to begin slowing down as soon as the sensors get close enough to the planet to begin receiving data."

"Good idea," agreed Ben. "It wouldn't help anyone if we just went charging into an unknown situation and got captured or hurt."

"Yes. What's the Unimind we are supposed to beware of?" Anita asked.

"Aristotle, play the transmission again," Tom asked.

The three friends spent the rest of the brief trip discussing what they might find on the mysterious planet. They listened to the distress signal over and over but were unable to pick up any new clues from it.

All at once, Tom felt the *Exedra* begin to slow. Before he could say anything, Aristotle announced, "Initial data now being received by the sensors."

"Put it on visual, maximum magnification," Tom ordered.

"I can detect no major metropolitan population centers as yet," Aristotle reported. "However, I am picking up some faint ground-communication signals. Can we perhaps drop to a lower orbit? I am curious because the language of the transmissions seems to be binary."

"It's as good as done," said Tom. He adjusted

the ship's altitude controls slightly, and the *Exedra*'s nose dipped toward the atmosphere.

"The gravity of the planet is one point two five the gravity of Earth," Ben remarked, his eyes glued to the data screen. "Atmosphere, oxygen-nitrogen with a high hydrocarbon level. That could mean some sort of industry or a lot of rotting vegetation—heavy jungle, that sort of thing."

"Oh, no," Anita groaned, screwing up her face in a grimace of mock distress. "If the gravity is twenty-five percent heavier than Earth's, that means I'm going to weigh, let's see . . . twenty-eight more pounds!"

"Tell us the truth," Ben kidded the slender young woman. "It was you who sneaked in and ate the leftover chocolate cake the other night! Now you're going to try and pass it off as heavier gravity. Shame, shame!"

"Look!" Tom shouted, pointing to the front port.

The young people all stared in awe at the planet below. It was a delicate jade-green sphere with swirls of white and brown hanging against the black backdrop of space.

"It's beautiful!" Anita gasped. "I wish there was some way to capture those magnificent colors in a necklace."

"Say what you want to about deep space, it has some of the most beautiful sights I've ever seen," Ben agreed.

"Movement!" Tom exclaimed. "Looks like there is something down there after all!"

Four bullet-nosed objects had pierced the atmosphere and were headed toward the *Exedra*.

"We've got a welcoming committee," Ben said.

Tom studied the approaching objects for a moment. "They're ships!" he cried. "Try to contact them, Ben."

"They sure are shaped funny," Anita commented.

Tom had to agree. The four vessels had fanned out in different directions and were converging on the *Exedra*. Much of their detail was now visible.

"I once had a perfume bottle shaped like that," said Anita thoughtfully. "It had a rounded black cap and the sides tapered toward the bottom exactly like those ships."

"The section behind the nose cone looks like it could be the drive housing. But that leaves very little space for life-support systems," Tom mused.

"Maybe the pilots are really tiny," Ben suggested.

"For some reason, since the planet is so much like Earth, I assumed the inhabitants would be pretty much like humans," Anita said. "I guess I was wrong. No human could fit into that kind of ship."

Abruptly, the smooth, shiny nose cones of the ships parted into four sections. They slowly opened like the petals of enormous black flowers. The centers contained clusters of what looked like sensors and cameras.

"There goes my theory about the passenger sections," Tom said.

Two huge portals dilated on each side of the ships, and metallic waldoes with wicked-looking metal claws were extended into space. Just below the sensor clusters, underbelly panels slid back to reveal backs of what appeared to be rocket launchers. The black-tipped warheads reflected the starlight ominously.

"Those ships are not acknowledging our signals," said Ben, frowning.

"Could they be drone ships?" Anita asked, a tiny bit of fear showing in her question.

"It would take enormously sophisticated equipment to control ships like that from the ground," replied Tom.

Suddenly, Aristotle spoke for the first time since his request to move the *Exedra* closer to the mysterious planet.

"They are not ships," the mechanoid said.

"They are robots. They are ordering us to land on the planet's surface."

"What?" asked Tom. "Why do they want us to land?"

"Tom, they are not replying to any of our questions," the robot continued. "They merely repeat their instructions. If we do not obey quickly, they will destroy us!"

Chapter Two

"What!" Tom exclaimed. The young inventor did not know which was more unbelievable—the fact that the ships were really robots, or their threats.

"Robots?" Ben asked.

"The robots are serious, Tom," Aristotle said.

They peered at the four objects. Numerous sinister-looking extensions were telescoping out of the bodies of the ships, and were pointing directly at the *Exedra!*

"They are transmitting in binary, Tom," Aristotle said. "But the language is still unknown to me. Wait, I am beginning to understand a bit of it now."

The robot was silent for a moment as he listened intently to the signals coming from the surrounding robots.

"Binary," Ben said ruefully to Tom. "That's one thing you didn't program into your translator unit!"

"I will, though, just as soon as Aristotle—"

"They are giving us our final chance to obey," Aristotle broke in. "It is *not* a request."

"Uh-oh," Ben muttered under his breath.

"I must say that I narrowly averted them attacking us just now," Aristotle added. "Maybe I am good for something after all."

Despite their dangerous situation, Tom and Ben could not help rolling their eyes heavenward. Aristotle's odd belief that he was in some way flawed had a habit of surfacing at the strangest times! Both boys had spent considerable time going over the robot's circuits, but neither of them had been able to locate the source of his inferiority complex.

"Well," Tom asked. "Where do they want us to set down?"

Aristotle spoke a set of coordinates as he programed them directly into the ship's onboard navigational computer.

"I don't think we have much choice right now, do we?" Tom commented. "Let's go."

The young people were silent as the *Exedra* began to spiral down. Tom studied the robots on the screens as they escorted them. With Aristotle's help, Ben began to program as much of the robots' binary language as he could into the TTU. Anita kept coming up with possible answers to their situation.

"The robots could be some kind of sophisticated defense system, controlled from the planet," she said.

No one had a better explanation.

"Is that a city?" Anita suddenly asked, pointing out one of the ports. "Or is it just a rock formation?"

A thick jungle spread across the land ahead, but there were two cleared spaces. One was a vast landing field toward which they were headed, a grayish concrete area with a strip of what appeared to be maintenance facilities along one edge.

Farther east was another cleared space in the green carpet of jungle. It was filled with many buildings, none more than three or four stories high. The entire city, as far as the three friends could see, was laid out in a rigid, square design.

"It is a city!" Ben exclaimed. "Wow! People!"

"No, maybe not *people*, but at least intelligent entities," Tom answered reasonably.

The landing itself was uneventful. The escorting robot ships set down at precisely the same time as the humans, except for one. That one took a position directly above the *Exedra* to prevent any last-minute escape.

"The atmosphere is breathable," Ben reported. "It's a touch high on nitrogen, but nothing to worry about. Pollen count five point one percent above Earth normal. And, of course, you feel the extra gravity already."

"Uh-huh," grunted Anita in annoyance. She got up from her contour couch and made a face. "Oh, *my!*"

"You'll get used to it," Tom comforted her. "Aristotle, anything?"

"They are requesting us to unfold the *Exedra*."

"Unfold?" Tom asked, puzzled. "Oh, they think this ship is like theirs. Have you told them?"

"Yes," the robot replied. "May I say, however, they do not have much in the way of manners. I do not believe they mean to be rude, but their requests and suggestions come across as orders."

Ben asked, "Shall we arm ourselves?"

Tom shook his head. "Hand weapons against

that?" he asked, gesturing to the outside. "They would not be very effective."

As they moved to the airlock, Aristotle asked, "Tom, may I make a suggestion?"

At the young inventor's nod, the robot said, "Allow me to go first."

Tom gestured Aristotle ahead of the three young people and they began the airlock cycle.

The first thing that struck them about the mysterious planet was its smell: machine oil and rotting vegetation mixed with the hot air of a tangy odor they could not identify.

Aristotle preceded them out of the airlock, and Tom had to step out before he could see around the mechanoid's bulk to what awaited them.

Two of the robot ships were close by, all the waldoes and turrets turned in their direction. Before them stood twelve odd metallic figures of differing sizes, shapes, and colors. They wore strange armor, and were all robots.

Some had wheels, others had legs or tracks like heavy earth-moving equipment on Earth. Some were short, squat, and brutal-looking. Others were tall and spindly. Still others were medium-sized, but there wasn't a friendly-looking face anywhere!

"Uh-oh," Ben said.

The humans had their TTU translators, and when a squat blue robot with a cluster of dull red eyes began to speak, they understood it.

"Why did you come here?" he demanded.

Tom started to respond, but Aristotle cut him off. A series of beeps and static filled the air.

Tom realized his mechanoid had spoken with incredible speed. The TTU, giving it to him in English, lagged far behind.

"We are from Earth. We were testing an interstellar drive when we entered your sphere of control," Aristotle explained.

Tom looked at Ben with alarm. They both had the same idea: perhaps the stardrive would have been better kept a secret!

There was another burst of beeps and pops. "You will go to the Unimind to be interviewed," the robot instructed.

"Unimind, huh?" Tom said to his friends. Instantly they remembered the warning portion of the distress signal, ". . . beware the Unimind."

They were marched down a ramp to a wheeled vehicle waiting at the bottom. It was obviously a cargo hauler, a flatbed on wheels with a control mechanism the size of a watermelon in front. Tom and his friends climbed aboard, but Aristotle did not.

"Come on," Tom said to his robot.

"It is best I go with them," Aristotle replied, gesturing to the robots beside him.

Bell bleep pop dink bleep! "Why do you confer with organisms?" the blue robot demanded.

"I was requesting permission to transport myself with the rest of you," Aristotle replied.

Bleep bleep pop click bleep!

Ponk bleep bleep dink pop snap blink!

"Requesting permission from biological organisms!" As flat as the TTUs made the robots' voices, it was clear they were all thoroughly shocked and outraged by Aristotle's actions.

A swift exchange of words followed which left the TTUs far behind. But the fact that the robots were confused was plain. Clearly, they did not understand how any machine intelligence could possibly submit itself to a biological unit.

Suddenly, one robot reached out an arm with three long metal fingers at the end. Quickly, it seized Anita, almost toppling the girl over as it raised her artificial lower leg.

"Hey!" the redhead protested.

Tom and Ben helped her get a better balance so that she would not fall. By then, more robots had clustered around her. They deftly removed her boot and sock, exposing the artificial leg which joined the flesh just below the knee.

The robots totally ignored both Anita's squirms and the boys' protests as they thumped and poked the leg.

Tom could tell from Anita's flaming face that she was very embarrassed. It was one thing for her friends to know that a childhood accident had caused part of her leg to be amputated. But it was quite another matter to have it so blatantly displayed in public!

The three young people listened to the swift exchange of robot language between Aristotle and what Tom was rapidly beginning to suspect were their captors.

All at once, they released Anita's leg, threw her boot and sock in her direction, and began to leave. The cargo hauler started in the direction of the city with the robots running, rolling, or riding next to the automatic craft.

Anita remained silent as she replaced her sock and boot, but Tom could tell she was fighting to control her emotions. He remembered Anita's earlier statement that they were headed for trouble. Was she receiving more emotional transmissions from this mysterious place? he wondered. He decided to let her alone for a while. If she was getting any important clues, she would let her friends know.

Tom looked around and noticed that the road

to the city was as straight as a ruler. The impression of a rigid grid, which is how the city had looked from the sky, was certainly borne out by the road they were now traveling.

The outskirts of the city were strange. The jungle abruptly stopped at the edge of a vast square of buildings, with no land in between, as on Earth. There were no fields, parks, or suburban houses.

The first buildings were odd-shaped to the humans' eyes. They reminded Tom of the plastic covering used to wrap products on Earth— vacuum-formed over the item on a flat card. There were lumps, domes, squares, cones, and facets. Each building was painted a flat gray with some kind of thick coating.

As they moved toward what seemed to be the center of the town, the buildings underwent a subtle change. The gray gave way to lighter colors, and some buildings had a contrasting trim. There was even a red, white, and blue dome! But the greatest change was in the shapes of the structures. Instead of the free-flowing, organic shapes they had first seen, the structures were now more rectangular. Windows began to appear, then even porches.

On the streets, entering and leaving the buildings, was the greatest collection of robots any of the young people had ever seen. There were a few giants, two or three times the height of an average human, and some not much bigger than a shoebox. There were spherical ones with a dozen tentacles of steel. There were long ones like tank cars, and medium-sized ones like two-, four-, six-, eight-, and even ten-legged creatures.

Steps instead of ramps were a feature of the inner city. There were also streetlights which had not been seen before.

"This is all more to human scale," Tom commented to his friends. "Look at the sizes of the doors in this part of town. In the outskirts they are so much bigger."

"This must be the oldest part of town," Anita agreed. "Then some kind of change took place and society underwent an enormous transformation."

"So, as the city expanded, it took on a different look," Ben added.

"I would guess that the robots took over from humans, or humanlike inhabitants. Then, as the mechanoids gained control, the city began to reflect their needs," Tom suggested.

"That would seem to go along with the distress

message," Ben said. "But where are the humans? I haven't seen anything but robots."

"I hope we're not too late to help them," Anita said.

"Tom," Ben said, his voice both quiet and urgent.

Tom glanced toward his Indian friend and saw something that seemed out of character with the rest of the city. On the street corners were huge sewer entrances, apparently built to cope with the heavy rains caused by the planet's climate. However, these entrances had been hastily blocked with large chunks of broken concrete paving, giving them an untidy appearance. Otherwise, the city was extremely neat. Too perfect, in fact. There were no leaves lying on the street, no newspapers blowing, no food wrappers, or any kind of refuse anywhere.

"I don't know what it means," Tom muttered to his friends under his breath, "but I'd be willing to bet a pint of real ice cream it's important."

"Notice the big pipes that come out of the ground?" Ben asked. "I think there is some kind of climate control here. I bet the robots have a rust problem with the humidity in the air."

He gestured at a facility they were passing. "See the distortion in the heat waves? The mechanoids must be refrigerating a *huge* area underground!"

"What I don't like is the way they looked at my leg!" Anita burst out. "I thought they were going to pull it off."

"Something that is only part machine and part biological must confuse them quite a bit," Tom commented.

"Why?" Ben asked. "We're all part machine. I've got fillings in my teeth. Someday I might wear glasses or use a hearing aid or have a piece of plastic in my gut."

"I'm just glad Anita's got a plastic leg with a computer inside," Tom broke in. "It's helped us out of jams before and I wouldn't be surprised if it did so again."

Before anyone could comment, the cargo hauler stopped abruptly, tumbling its human passengers. They untangled themselves and looked at the building in front of them.

It was the only mirrored structure they had seen so far. In the wall before them they could see themselves reflected—surrounded by a dozen robots.

"Enter!" commanded the blue mechanoid who seemed to be giving all the orders.

The young people went in rather cautiously.

They stared around, trying to find clues which would give them some grasp of the civilization that had built this city.

And what had happened to the beings who had sent the distress signal?

Had Tom and his friends arrived too late to help them?

Chapter Three

The walls surrounding Tom, Ben, and Anita were completely mirrored, and around the entrance area was a border of carved leaves, the only decoration they had seen so far in this world.

"Is this some kind of exhibit?" Ben wondered aloud.

On the left was a cluster of clear plastic tubes, some only a few feet high, others going almost to the top of the enormous lobby.

Anita's eyes traveled to the ceiling above them. "It must be thirty or forty feet high!" she exclaimed.

The tubes, which ranged in diameter from the

size of a pencil to about twelve feet, were filled with brightly colored liquids. Inside the liquid were seashells, sand, and pebbles. Other tubes contained chunks of natural-looking crystals and golden ball bearings. Some even had pieces of dried vegetation!

"What on earth do you make of this?" Ben asked.

"It's not on Earth, so I have no idea," Tom quipped.

His friends groaned.

To the right was a different sort of display. At first, the young people thought it was a delegation of officials. But as they looked more closely, they realized it was a grotesque graveyard for deactivated robots. Each had been painted a flat black—even across its lenses and sensors!

"It reminds me of the Museum of Natural History," Anita said, "where they have exhibits like 'The Development of the Horse,' 'The Fossil Remains of the Dinosaurs,' 'The Development of Man,' that sort of thing."

"Look!" Tom exclaimed. "It goes from right to left. The earliest ones were bipedal, had two arms, and were about our size. Then they became specialized, like insects. Multi-armed, taller or shorter, depending on what their job was . . ."

"And *Robotus Giganticus*, back there." Ben

pointed to a unit in the rear which was easily twenty-five feet tall. "Looks like a wrestler— long arms, thick body. Obviously very strong."

The shrill beepings from their blue robot guide stopped their musings. "I think he wants us to move on," Tom said.

They followed him across the lobby into another mirrored hall and up a ramp. Through an open arch they saw an aquarium.

"Hold it a minute," said Ben and tapped their guide on the shoulder.

The wall of the aquarium was also the wall of the room. It contained clear water without fish of any sort, but the bottom seemed to be a replica of an ocean bottom. Rocks, sand, and tiny clusters of crystals were scattered all over.

A spherical vessel floated inside the tank.

"Maybe it's a totally new kind of robot," Ben suggested.

The small machine was quickly and agilely picking up nodules of minerals from the bottom with four tiny waldoes extending from its lower part. Each nugget was lifted to the top of the robot and deposited into a hole. In seconds, all the nodules were gathered up. The top hatch of the undersea robot snapped shut, water was pumped out, and the machine popped toward the surface.

It was climbing out as another load of nodules was dumped into the tank. A second undersea mechanism dropped into the tank with a foam of air bubbles. It was similar to, but not identical with, the first harvester.

"This must be a testing tank," Anita said.

"Can robots look impatient without moving?" Ben asked their guide.

He did not answer.

"If they can't, then this one is doing a very good imitation of it," Anita commented.

"This must be an important building for the robots," Tom said as they followed the blue mechanoid through more corridors. "It's probably central headquarters."

"Why do you say that?" Ben asked.

"Firstly, it's the only building we've seen which has mirrors. It seems to be in the center of the city and it contains, among other things, an exhibit of the robots' history. Plus those tanks mean it's a testing or learning center," Tom explained.

"But where are the people who built it?" Anita asked. "Did *they* put the dead robots in the building or did the robots?"

"Have you seen anyone but robots here?" Ben asked, concern in his voice. "I haven't noticed a thing that looks even vaguely humanoid. I hope we're not too late."

Before the others could reply, they turned a corner and found a crowd of white-bodied, multi-armed mechanoids coming toward them. They were knee-high, and their sensors were waving from the ends of extended stalks. They clustered around Anita. The young girl started to blush as they examined her closely.

"Hey, get away from her!" Tom shouted.

They looked startled. All motion stopped and their eyestalks swiveled toward Tom and Ben.

"Go on!" Ben snapped, waving his arms at them.

The eyestalks snapped back into their white bodies and the robots' limbs closed in tightly. They simply squatted, motionless, until Tom, Ben, and Anita had gone.

"They certainly are interested in your leg, all right!" Tom said to the redhead. She nodded, still looking embarrassed.

The three young people passed through areas in which there were no halls, just open complexes of rooms. Some were filled with blue cubes or yellow, many-sided figures. Others contained silver balls or green cones. There were areas in which a robot stood absolutely motionless, or identical units faced each other in a circle.

"What are we getting into?" Ben muttered. "I've never seen anything so alien before—so mechanical-looking and dead. It's scary!"

"I agree," Tom replied. "Even though the Skree's world was alien, at least it was alive. This one's awfully sterile. Which is quite a feat for being in the middle of a jungle!"

"Frankly, I'd feel more comfortable in the jungle," Anita put in.

A huge, squat robot had joined the small procession. Tom decided not to hide his annoyance at the way he and his friends were being treated, yet his suspicion that they were prisoners was growing every second. "Are you the Unimind?" Tom demanded of the new robot. "They told us we were going to meet the Unimind. So far, all I've seen since we landed have been flunky robots!" There was no reply.

Tom turned away and then added as an afterthought, "Incidentally, it's way too cold in here, so you'd better turn the air conditioning off!" He rubbed his arms and shuddered for emphasis, even though he did not expect his demand to be complied with.

He guessed the temperature inside the building to be somewhere in the low sixties. That would mean there was bound to be a bank of computers nearby, since they needed low temperatures to operate.

There were clicking and whirring sounds Tom's TTU could not translate. The robot's sensorframe blinked repeatedly. Tom guessed it was the robot's version of a shocked reaction to his order.

"Tom!" Anita hissed. "What are you doing?"

"Trust me," was all Tom said. He could not tell his friends that their only hope might lie in keeping the robots guessing about the unpredictability of true human nature.

"When I receive the proper code, you will be taken to the Unimind," the robot suddenly told him in a flat voice.

"Until then, what about the air conditioning?" Tom persisted. This time, Ben raised his eyebrows warningly.

"Optimum temperature must be maintained for proper functioning," the machine replied. "Climate-control settings cannot be altered to suit biological organisms."

It seemed to Tom that the words "biological organisms" were spoken with a hint of contempt.

The twelve robot guards, who had not left them since they had gotten out of the cargo hauler, made several clicking noises, but the TTUs did not translate. Tom began to worry that perhaps something was wrong with the units.

However, since they seemed to function when the young people were spoken to directly, he decided it was not too serious.

The corridor curved sharply and then began winding in tight "S" curves. Suddenly, it widened into a chamber filled with machinery and robots who moved and clicked furiously.

Tom recognized some of the pieces as chemical-analysis equipment, but the others were alien to him. None of the busy mechanoids paid any attention to the party as it passed through.

"We've been going steadily uphill," Ben panted. "And walking in the heavier gravity is beginning to get to me."

"Me too!" Anita agreed. "Thank goodness it's air-conditioned in here. I'd hate to do all this hiking in the jungle outside! But it's so chaotic! I can't keep any sense of direction."

"I can't, either," Tom agreed. "But at the same time it's very logical. The robots have defined their space according to necessity. Think of it as a beehive. Like bees, the robots have no desire for privacy, the way we do."

"You're right," Ben exclaimed. "On Earth our space needs to be clearly defined. I remember how happy I was when my parents gave me my own room. Everything inside those four walls was mine! But that would mean nothing to a robot."

Anita leaned toward her friends and lowered her voice. "Have you noticed the last few groups we have passed all seem to be working on something they are in a big hurry to complete?"

"They've been busy," Ben responded, "but I haven't noticed any panic on their part."

"No, not panic," Anita said. "But I'm picking up a very strong sense of urgency. Odd," she paused for a moment, "I didn't realize I could get emotions from machines."

"Perhaps they're not coming from the robots. Maybe they're coming from someplace else," Tom suggested.

The lead robot's motorframe continued to roll forward, but the sensorframe rotated to look at Anita. The gesture chilled her!

And it reminded Tom of Aristotle. Where was he? Why had he not joined them yet? Had the robots done something to harm him?

"Just what do you and your fellow mechanoids have against biological organisms?" Anita asked the lead robot. "You were probably built by one!"

"That does not compute!" the machine intoned. "I was brought to awareness by the

MK-140 master circuit ten cycles ago. I can trace my development through three prototypes, five upgradings, and fourteen working models since the conception. My level of sophistication is beyond any engineering capabilities of organic intelligence!"

A row of tiny orange indicator lights on the top of the robot's sensorframe flashed on and off, as if in anger.

"Whew! Whole generations of robots built by other robots!" Ben whistled softly through his teeth.

"That means they've had plenty of time to corrupt their original programing," Tom observed.

"From the way they react to us, they've done a pretty thorough job of it," Anita agreed.

"It's obvious they have tried to blot out their origins," Ben observed. "But you can't deny that their lights, indicators, and sensor-access panels are design traditions going back to the days of the beings who built them. Robots don't need those things to communicate with each other."

Just then, the group entered a vast chamber. *Bleep wee opp pop pop bleep!* the lead robot said, and the twelve guards began conversing rapidly. The TTUs translated all the sounds at once, which resulted in total confusion. Tom put his hands over his ears to cut out the noise.

Without warning, one guard extended an evil-looking, three-pincered hook and grabbed Anita's right arm.

"Cut that out!" the beautiful redhead yelled. "You're hurting me!"

The robot seemed not to care. Another mechanoid firmly took Anita's other arm and the two dragged the struggling girl down the corridor toward what appeared to be a solid wall!

Tom and Ben raced after them.

"Let go of her!" Tom shouted and ran in front of the robots. They made no move to get out of his way, but rolled right at the young inventor.

Tom threw all the weight of his solidly built six-foot frame against one of them with his best body block. But he was knocked to the floor!

Ben slammed two tightly balled fists into the indicator lights and sensors of the robot nearest him. "If I can just do some damage—" he grunted, but one of the guards rammed an arm into his solar plexis, sending the young Indian flying across the chamber. He thudded against a wall and slid weakly to the floor. Blood trickled from the corner of his mouth from a split lip.

Meanwhile, the robots continued dragging Anita toward the solid-looking wall. With a heavy whoosh of air, a section of it slid back. Tom caught a brief glance of several strange alien plants.

Then the wall shut again with a resounding click—cutting off Anita's screams abruptly!

Chapter Four

"Come on!" Tom yelled, running toward the wall panel.

Ben struggled to his feet and limped over to join his friend.

"It's not pressure-activated from a floor plate," he said after a moment of examination.

The boys began feeling the now-solid wall carefully, but without success.

Tom whirled to face the robots. During all the excitement, they had stood silent, seemingly unaware of what was going on. "Where did they take her?" he shouted. "You'd better open that door or—" he paused, not knowing what he could say to threaten them with.

After a slight pause, the robot leader said, "As you wish."

The panel slid back mysteriously and Tom and Ben walked cautiously through the entrance.

"Biological organisms cannot dominate machine intelligence. It is unnatural," the robot said as the panel closed behind them.

They looked around anxiously, but Anita was nowhere to be seen.

"You realize now we're trapped, don't you?" Ben asked, wiping blood from his lip.

Tom nodded and stared at his environment. All around them, strange plants grew in tanks of soil and nutrients.

"Why would robots be experimenting with hydroponics?" he asked his friend.

Ben shrugged. "This is certainly the oddest plant life I've ever seen."

There were beautiful orange thistles with complicated, wormy-looking centers. Green melon-shaped plants, looking like Christmas ornaments with multicolored spikes and delicate hairy growths at their tops, had magenta cups filled with a smelly liquid. And all had one thing in common—all had small, weak-looking leaves.

"Ben," Tom muttered softly, "I have a feeling we are being watched." He scanned the room intently, but could not see any hidden cameras or sensors.

"The lighting in this chamber seems too unnatural to support plants," Ben said, pointing to the ceiling. "It's nothing like the light of any sun I've ever seen!"

Tom heard a sudden dry, rustling sound near him. He whirled, but saw no one in the hydroponics chamber except Ben and himself.

"Hello!" he called out.

There was no answer.

Slowly, the boys walked through the rows of tanks. Tom paused near a noxious purple, cactuslike plant with black spikes that were oozing a thick, gluey substance. He bent closer and noticed brown stains on a few of the spikes. Then he saw reddish blond hairs on the gluey substance!

"Anita's hair!" he exclaimed, and shuddered. The aisle in front of him was empty, but he could hear Ben's footsteps.

"Ben, come look at this!" he called out.

Suddenly, there was a violent rustling sound from plant stalks moving.

"Yaaaaaah! Let *go* of me!" Ben shouted.

"*Ben!*" Tom ran in the direction of his friend's voice. He rapidly turned a corner and stopped short in terror at what he saw!

The young Indian was locked in a fierce struggle with a green melon plant!

Its head had split into three sections that gripped Ben's arm near his shoulder. The boy was trying to pry the jaws of the fleshy green monstrosity open with his bare hands, all the while panting and gasping loudly for air. Sweat poured down his face and his muscles bulged with effort.

"Tom—help! The gravity—I'm so tired." Blood was running down the young technician's arm where the thorns—or teeth—of the plant had bitten it.

Tom grabbed the stalk of the plant. He felt the vertebrae move and twist in his grasp. "This thing is strong!" he muttered to himself. He, too, could feel the effects of the planet's heavy gravity pulling at him.

"Tom, these plants are carnivorous! It's dinnertime and we're dinner!" Ben shouted.

Eeennn! Eeennn! From all sides, the plants wove and bobbed with excitement. They emitted shrieks that Tom found even more frightening than the plants' actions.

Plants that make sounds? Well, this is an alien world, he told himself.

The young inventor stopped trying to break the stalk of the plant and began pulling with all his might. "I'm trying to uproot it!" he shouted to Ben.

Suddenly, there was more rustling near him and he looked up just in time to leap aside!

Three of the melon plants snapped at the air where he had stood only seconds before!

Tom wished fervently that he had some kind of weapon!

Eeeennnn! Eeennn! Thick juice bubbled from the wormlike mouths of the huge orange plants. The segments moved in and around each other spasmodically.

Tom felt a tugging at the leg of his jumpsuit. Looking down, he saw with horror that the long, fibrous tongue of a yellow brain plant was wrapping itself around his ankle! He kicked at it viciously and smashed the plant into a sickening pulp. It let out a high-pitched yelp that excited the carnivorous plant monsters even more.

Out of the corner of his eye, Tom saw another movement. He raised his arm to shield his face, just in time to avoid the pink-and-red lined mouth of an enormous black sunflower!

The hungry plant bit into the young inventor's wristwatch and jerked away, screaming in anger.

Tom abandoned all hope of uprooting the plant that had such an iron grip on Ben's arm. He doubled up his fists and began pounding on its head. But he was tiring and he could see Ben was, too.

"Hold . . . on . . . Ben!" the young inventor shouted. With his last bit of strength, he tried desperately to break the jaws of the plant. Thick, gluey liquid dripped onto his hand. It burned and he knew Ben's arm must be on fire from the stuff seeping into his open wounds.

Suddenly, he felt himself pushed aside, as if he were a child. Two huge hands with square fingers wrapped themselves around the melon plant!

As Tom stared in surprise, a muscular human-oid gripped the stalk firmly, and with a grunt, bent the neck of the plant. It gurgled with surprise and squirmed in his grasp. This did not seem to bother the mysterious stranger at all. With a quick twist, he broke the plant's neck in two.

The head part released its hold on Ben's arm and fell limply to the floor. The root end began oozing foul-smelling green bile.

All over the room, the monster plants screamed with rage. They wove and bobbed their heads and snapped their jaws, anxious for a chance to get at their new enemies.

"Th-thanks!" said Ben. He carefully probed his injured arm and winced when he touched an open wound.

The olive-skinned alien grinned and wiped his hands on his tattered jumper. Tom noticed that the material was a synthetic containing metallic fibers. He was surprised that the stranger wore such sophisticated clothing. Somehow, it did not seem to go with his shoulder-length reddish-blond hair secured with an Aztec-style headband.

"I am Ahn, Tor's son," said the alien. The translator-teacher units converted his words for Tom and Ben. "Come on, we'd better get out of here before the plants decide to get even!"

Tom and Ben followed him as he expertly wove in and out of the hydroponic tanks, taking care to stay out of reach of the carnivorous plants.

Ahn's height was not exceptional, but he was massive all over. Yet his bulk was not fat, Tom noticed. It was all muscle. His features were large and somewhat square. Tom thought Anita would probably think the alien was handsome in a rugged sort of way.

Anita! Where was she now? They had to find her!

Just then, Ahn pointed to a break in the wall in front of him. Tom and Ben watched him ease through, then they followed.

The first thing that struck Tom was how cool it felt. He had been so busy fighting off the plants that he had not noticed the heat in the hydroponics room. It had been at least fifteen degrees warmer than the adjoining chamber. And even there, the temperature was much above that in the hallways.

Apparently, the robots had outfitted the plant room with a special temperature sensor. The mechanoids themselves would rust quickly in the warm, humid climate. This thought brought the young inventor back to the question he had asked Ben earlier.

"Why do the robots have a hydroponics room?" he asked once again.

"Robots?" Ahn asked. Then understanding flooded his face. "Oh, you mean the Metal Ones."

He paused for a moment. "What are they called in your world?"

"Robots," Tom repeated.

Ben looked at their rescuer. "What kind of life can you have on this planet with those plants around?"

"There aren't any others," Ahn replied. "These are just the result of a failed experiment. The metal ones—uh, the robots—never stop thinking of clever ways to kill us."

The young alien's face grew dark as he continued. "They spent a lot of time and effort growing those plants here, but when they took them out of the special room, the roots rotted."

Tom glanced around the chamber they were in now. It was small and completely empty.

"How did you get here?" Ahn asked the two boys. "And where are you from?"

"We came to this planet in, er. . . ." Tom paused for a moment, wondering how he would explain the concept of a spaceship to Ahn. "We came in a ship which travels through the sky from another world, like this one, far, far away— up there." He pointed at the ceiling.

Ahn looked at the boys curiously for a moment and then nodded.

"Why are you here?" Tom asked. "You are the first humanoid being we've seen."

"As far as I know, I'm the only surviving member of a scouting party. We tried to sneak into the city to spy on the Metal Ones. But we didn't get very far," Ahn explained.

"We came to this planet in response to a broadcasted message of distress," Ben spoke up. "Did your people send it?"

"I don't know," Ahn replied. "There are old stories that say there are machines in the sky asking for help. But who built the machines, or how they got in the sky, is a mystery."

Tom and Ben exchanged surprised glances.

"How long have your people been fighting the robots?" Ben asked.

"Why, always!" Ahn seemed surprised by the question. "That is how it has been for as long as anyone can remember."

"Didn't you ever live in the city?" Tom asked. "Didn't you build it?"

Ahn's face began to darken again, and the young inventor realized he had asked a touchy question without meaning to do so. "There are many old stories, but that is all they are, old stories!" Ahn said stiffly. "What is real is that the robots would do away with my people if they could. That is why we spy on them, to try and discover what new terrors they have in store for us."

The alien looked around the room, as if searching for a way to escape which he might have, somehow, overlooked before.

"The Metal Ones—uh, robots—are working on something new and very big. That much we learned before being captured. They are in a great hurry to use it on us." He sighed in frustration. "This building is the key to their plans. Now I'll never be able to warn my people about it!"

"Anita was sure there was something special going on, too, although I don't know how she could get empathic impressions from robots," Ben said.

"Do you know how long you've been here?" Tom asked.

The alien shook his head. "Several days, I suppose. We tried to escape just after the, uh, robots took us prisoner and put us in here. We made that hole in the wall to break out of the special room with the plants, but that's as far as we got. The robots have taken us, one by one. I am the only one left now. I have no idea what they have done with the others."

"We have two friends somewhere in the city and we have to find them!" Tom exclaimed.

Ahn shook his head. "I am afraid you may as well give up on them," he said sadly.

Chapter Five

"What do you mean?" Tom asked, concern in his voice.

"Once the robots take people, they are never seen again. No one knows what happens to them, but they are gone forever. That is how it has always been." The young alien looked truly sorry to be telling Tom and Ben such bad news.

"But have you actually seen Anita or Aristotle?" Tom asked anxiously.

"No. You two are the only strangers I have ever encountered," Ahn replied. "But your friends are gone forever. I am sure of it."

"I don't think so," the young inventor insisted. "They're both pretty clever."

"Meanwhile, we've got to get ourselves out of here!" Ben said.

"It's time to clean out the old pockets," Tom said. "One nice thing about these robots, they're not curious, like us organic types. They're not at all suspicious."

He noticed Ahn's look of puzzlement. "They have no knowledge of Earth humans as yet and so they don't know what to expect from us," he explained. "That's why the pockets of our jump-suits weren't searched."

"Hurray for dumb guards!" Ben exclaimed.

Ahn watched, fascinated, as the two young humans reached into every pocket of their suits and placed the contents on the floor.

Ben looked at his small collection. "My ring of keys, a pocket comb, some theater stubs for *Pride of the Space Fleet*—don't bother to see it when we get back, it's dull—a paper clip, some change, and my handkerchief. Not much help there," he said regretfully. "What have you got?"

"My notebook, a ball-point pen, keys, a broken wristwatch, handkerchief, and half a pack of gum," replied Tom.

"Hey, you've been holding out on me," the young computer tech exclaimed. "I'm hungry."

"Now that you mention it, I am, too," said Tom.

"But forget about the gum. It'll stimulate your appetite even more."

"What I wouldn't give for a nice, juicy steak, done medium rare, with a huge baked potato just dripping with real butter and sour cream oozing all over, and maybe—"

"Enough!" Tom said. "Don't make it worse than it already is."

The young man began to pace slowly around the room, his mind obviously considering and then rejecting various ideas. "If we can get the robots to open a door, either in this room or in the hydroponics room, maybe we could rush them. Flesh is still quicker than steel."

"We thought of that already," Ahn said. "We pounded on the walls for lengthy time periods and they never came except when they took one of us away. Once in a while they brought us water."

"You mean you've had no food since you got here?" asked Ben.

"No. I had forgotten my hunger until you arrived," the alien replied.

"Sorry," said Ben.

Tom picked up the package of gum and looked at it thoughtfully. Then he turned and crawled back through the hole in the wall into the hydroponics room. At once, the plants began chattering excitedly. Ben poked his head through the hole and frowned at his friend. "Are you crazy, Tom?" he asked.

"The climate in here is carefully regulated," Tom said. "That means there's a temperature sensor connected to some kind of thermostat. Come in here. You, too, Ahn. I need your help."

Tom pulled out three sticks of gum. He gave one to Ben, one to Ahn, and unwrapped the third piece and popped it into his mouth. "Chew," he commanded.

Ben obliged, but the puzzled expression never left his face.

Ahn watched the two humans. His eyes grew wide as he began chewing the sweet, rubbery gum. He swallowed loudly.

"Hey!" Tom protested. "You're not supposed to swallow it! Here. Be careful with this," he said as he handed Ahn another piece of gum. "This is my last piece. Just chew it until I tell you to stop."

Everyone chewed in silence for a few minutes, then Tom held out his hand. "Okay, give it to me."

He pulled his own piece of gum out of his mouth and wadded the three pieces together.

Ben watched his friend for a minute before he finally burst out, "Mind telling me what this is all about? Maybe I could help!"

Tom searched the room with his eyes, trying to notice every detail. "The sensor has to be exposed," he said.

Ben's face lit up and he, too, began searching. Ahn looked very puzzled by the strange actions of the two young humans.

"Over there," said Tom, pointing across the room. "See that little bump on the wall? I bet that's it!"

"Do we have to go through those plants again?" Ben asked worriedly.

"If we stick close to the wall, they won't get us. I'll put the wad of gum over the sensor. It's going to send an alarm to the monitoring equipment and one of the robots will have to come to check it. When the door opens, we've got to be ready!"

"That sounds like a reasonable plan. If I think of a better one, I'll be sure to mention it," Ben said, grinning at his friend.

"I knew I could count on you!" said Tom, slapping him on the back playfully.

"Ouch!" hissed Ben. "Don't forget I was almost some plant's dinner."

"Sorry," Tom apologized.

The young inventor molded the sticky gum until it completely covered the heat sensor. Then he carefully edged his way over to the wall panel, where Ben and Ahn were standing. "That's it. Now we wait."

They were quiet for several minutes, and just listened. No robots came.

"I hate to say this, ol' buddy, but I think your plan is a bust," Ben declared finally. "That's all right, though, I couldn't have done any better."

"Don't give up yet," Tom said. "Look!" He pointed at the plants. Something was happening to them. The viscous green melons were turning a paler green and some of the deadly flowers were beginning to wither on their stalks.

"It's already getting colder in here," Ben exclaimed excitedly. "If the robots don't hurry, the plants will all die. Personally, I wouldn't consider that a great loss, but—"

"Shhh!" hissed Tom, putting his ear to the wall.

The next instant, the panel slid open and a squat mechanoid entered the chamber.

Ahn was crouched, ready to spring, but Ben pushed the young alien back.

"Aristotle!" Tom exclaimed.

"There is not much time," the robot said, "so please listen carefully. When I left you, I was taken to the library. I have spent most of my time learning about the history of this planet and about the robot civilization. With all their weapons and knowledge, they are not as sophisticated as I am. I suspected this from the beginning and so, unfortunately, did they."

Ben started to interrupt, but Aristotle held up a metal hand and continued.

"Their hostility toward me has been thinly disguised. They are all on a central link. As soon as one robot knows something, they all know it. My circuitry allows me to keep my programing and sensor data private. That is disturbing them and they are growing more and more insistent that I be linked up to the Unimind."

"There's that word again," Ben said.

"So we've got to find Anita and escape at once!" Tom cried out.

"I am afraid there is something more urgent than that," the robot told him. He turned to Ahn.

"I regret to inform you that your three companions died as a result of experiments conducted by the robots. The experiments were successful, in other words."

"What do you mean?" asked Tom.

"The robots have been working on a chemical to exterminate all organic life on this planet. They have found the right formula—and they plan to use it very soon!"

Chapter Six

"If what you say is true, I must alert the village immediately!" Ahn cried. "We must mount an attack on the city!"

"That is correct," Aristotle agreed.

"How do I know I can trust your information?" the alien asked suspiciously. "You *are* a robot!"

"I built Aristotle," said Tom. "He'd have to circumvent all my programing to lie to you. He would be hurting me, too, and I programed him to be absolutely loyal."

"I was able to locate you by your TTU," the mechanoid went on. "Others are on their way here. I am going to help you escape so that you can warn Ahn's people."

"What about Anita?" asked Tom anxiously.

"That is where I hope to redeem myself for my flaws," the robot said. "You will not be able to find her, and if you try, it will result in your being killed. Then everyone will die. Right now I have access to information on her and I shall endeavor to keep her safe until your return. That is the least I can do after getting you into this situation."

Tom sighed in frustration. Sometimes Aristotle's inferiority complex got on the young inventor's nerves. "It's not your fault," Tom said. "And you certainly don't have to redeem yourself from anything. I wish you'd cut all that out!"

"If I were not such a flawed mechanism, maybe I could 'cut it out,' as you say," Aristotle replied. "But come, we are wasting time."

Tom, Ben, and Ahn followed him out of the plants' chamber. Tom looked back once more and saw that the green melon plants were now almost white and their heads hung limply from their stalks. Green bile slowly dripped from their jaws. The shorter purple cactus plants were brown and withered. The young inventor smiled.

Aristotle closed the wall panel behind them. "After I located you, I checked the schematic of this building. It was constructed on the site of the old science complex, the one Ahn's people, the Karshe, built."

Ahn whirled toward Aristotle. "My people . . . built *this?*" He gestured in amazement at the buildings around them.

"Of course," Aristotle said, ignoring the sense of wonder in the young alien's voice.

"You said—*that* word. The word you called my people," Ahn continued.

"Karshe," Aristotle repeated. "That is the name of your people."

Tom and Ben looked at each other, puzzled. The young inventor wished they had time to stay and straighten out a lot of things, but they had already lost valuable time and needed to hurry if they were going to escape.

"Look," he said, "I really have to interrupt this conversation. It's obvious Aristotle has discovered a lot of history about this place that the robots have been suppressing for years, but right now we've got to get out of here."

"You are right, Tom. Once again, I have proved what a flawed—" Aristotle began.

"Aristotle! Get us out of here. NOW!" Tom ordered.

Aristotle began walking, but continued his lecture. "The robots incorporated the existing base structure into their architecture. If we follow this corridor—"

He paused for a moment, then looked at Tom with his camera "eyes."

"A maintenance crew is on its way to the hydroponics chamber. Once they discover you are missing, they will try to locate me. I can block their probes, of course, but for Anita's sake, I will have to let them find me eventually."

Tom put a reassuring hand on Aristotle's mainframe. "Listen, old friend. I don't want you to jeopardize your standing with the robots. Go back and pretend you don't know anything about our escape. We'll get along fine from here on. Now go!"

"If you insist," Aristotle said. "Take this passage until it ends and then use this device." He opened his circuit panel, produced a small electronic disk, and handed it to Tom. It was about the size of a quarter.

"Where did you get this?" the young inventor asked, turning it over in his hand.

"I made it," said Aristotle. "Forgive me, but I cannibalized some of my own minor circuits—nothing important, you understand. Still, I hesitated to tamper with your handiwork. But it was the only way I could make this device so quickly."

"But what is it, Aristotle?" Ben asked.

"It is the same gadget which the robots use to activate the wall panels. I knew you would need it to get out of the city—and to get back in, once you are ready to fight the robots."

Tom swallowed the lump in his throat and blinked in gratitude. "Thanks, pal," he said huskily.

Aristotle swiveled his sensorframe abruptly and began rolling back the way they had come. "Do not mention it, Tom," he called over his shoulder.

Ahn looked at him and then at Tom, with a puzzled expression on his face. Then he whirled and trotted down the corridor. Tom and Ben ran along with him. In a few minutes, they reached the end without having encountered any other robots. Tom slapped Aristotle's disk to the bare wall in front of them.

Nothing happened!

"It was a trick!" Ahn snorted.

Ben glanced over his shoulder to see if they were being followed yet. He knew time was running out fast.

Tom took the disk and turned it over in his fingers, thoughtfully. Then he put the opposite side against the wall.

Like magic, the panel slid back and the three young men darted through. Tom closed the panel behind them and they were thrust into darkness for a moment until their eyes adjusted to the dim light.

Tom gradually made out a steep metal stairway leading down. From below came the sound of rushing water and the echo of machinery.

"This leads to the sewers," Ahn exclaimed in wonder. Then the muscular alien frowned. "I don't know which is worse—fighting our way out of the city on the surface, or escaping through here!"

"Remember when we were being taken through the city and saw the concrete rubbish piled against the sewer entrances?" Ben asked Tom. "How will we get out of here?"

"The drainage exits are not blocked," said Ahn. "But we will have other worries soon." The alien started down the metal staircase without explaining himself. Tom and Ben followed him.

The trip was not a long one, but by the time Tom and Ben had reached the bottom, they were out of breath and sweating from the effort. Tom wondered if they would ever get used to the heavy gravity of Ourworld.

Suddenly, from deep within the cavernous sewer, they heard the heavy clanking of giant machinery.

Ahn frowned, concerned. "The sewer system is

controlled, somehow, from within the building," he said. "That much we have discovered during our spy missions. I am afraid we had better get out of this section, in case it is going to be flooded."

The muscular alien began walking carefully, staying close to the dingy, slimy walls. Tom and Ben did the same.

"Ech!" the young Indian said as his hands touched the walls for balance. "This place is really disgusting!"

Tom suspected that at one time the sewers were probably kept clean. But during the years of robot occupation, layers of silt and rock had built up inside the ducts. Now the young inventor and his friends were sloshing through foul-smelling black mud.

A narrow river of thick fluid was flowing swiftly down the center of the duct. Tom shuddered at the thought of slipping and falling in. He doubted he would be able to fight the current for very long in his weakened condition.

More clanks and booms of machinery echoed through the sewer, amplified by the construction of the chamber.

"Ben, is it my imagination, or is the water level rising?" Tom asked.

Ben peered at the dark, dangerous-looking

river beneath them. "I can't tell, but its speed has certainly increased," he said.

"Could the robots be trying to flood us out of here?" asked Tom.

"We'd better run," was Ahn's reply. "Watch your step, though." He nodded toward the rushing stream. Tom and Ben needed no caution about that!

The air was warm, moist, and heavy with strange odors. Some of the stink came from rotting vegetation, but Tom could also detect animal smells.

There was no doubt about it any more: the sewer water was rising rapidly!

Whether the robots were deliberately flooding the place or whether it was just an automatic cycling did not really matter. Death by drowning was death by drowning.

"Look!" Tom pointed in front of them. "This chamber branches out. I think we should take our chances and get out of the main area."

"I agree." Ben yelled. "We'll be swimming in here pretty soon."

"I suppose it's our only chance," Ahn agreed.

Tom was surprised at the muscular alien's sudden hesitation, but he forgot it when he saw what was happening ahead of them.

The two huge doors of the branching passage were beginning to slide shut!

"Hurry!" Tom screamed at his friends.

They began to run.

Suddenly, Tom was thrown off-balance. Something living dived between his legs, tripping him. He fell on his stomach in the mud and rolled. He felt the filthy mud splash onto his face and he shut his mouth and eyes tightly.

When he looked up, Ben and Ahn were disappearing into the branch duct, totally unaware that he was now lying in the mud. In the gloom, he saw the indistinct form of a dirty brown and black animal follow Ahn and Ben into the passage.

Tom jumped to his feet, shaking away the pain of his fall, and raced toward the doors. His heart skipped a beat. The opening was already too small for him to slip through!

He felt something wet around his ankles and looked down to see that the water level in the main chamber had already risen over his sneakers. The tug of the current was growing stronger, sucking at his feet.

"Tom!"

The young inventor suddenly heard Ben scream his name.

Then the doors of the branch passage banged shut with a heavy thud!

Tom looked around in desperation. He was trapped!

Chapter Seven

"Tom! Are you there? Tom! Answer me!" Ben's voice came muffled from the other side of the huge doors.

"Stay where you are!" Tom yelled to his friend. "I'll find high ground somewhere!"

He looked around, but the walls of the sewer were steep and smooth. The chamber had become noticeably higher the last forty or fifty feet and Tom could no longer see the ceiling.

He began splashing away from the wall. Progress was slow because the sewer water was now up to the middle of his calves. The current kept trying to take his legs out from under him. He squinted down the tunnel, trying to find a place where he would be safe from the water. But it was so dark that it was impossible to see more than a few feet in any direction.

Then, over the sound of the rushing stream, Tom heard a high-pitched, wailing sound. Was it a baby crying?

He strained to see through the darkness, then gave up and started following the sound.

Gradually, he moved closer, but he still could not see the source of the wailing. It seemed to be coming from above him. Now it no longer sounded like a baby. Actually, he thought, it sounds like a cat!

The water was now waist-deep, and it was almost impossible for Tom to keep his balance. He looked up and stared straight into two large green eyes. A fur-covered paw reached down from an opening in the wall and batted at him!

"It *is* a cat!" Tom cried. "A cat—*here*? Buddy, you just saved my life!"

With all the strength he could muster, he leaped up out of the water and grasped the edge of the ledge. The cat backed away, spitting and hissing, while Tom struggled to maintain his hold.

With his feet off the ground, there was no way the young inventor could resist the heavy current of the water. It pulled and tugged at him, trying to break his perilous grip on the ledge.

Tom took a deep breath. He felt his fingers slipping and knew he only had one chance to make it to safety. With the last bit of strength he could muster, he hauled himself inch by inch into the opening above his head. Then he lay still for several minutes, panting and choking.

Finally, he turned over. A large, dirty brown and black cat was staring at him warily.

"Nice kitty," Tom wheezed, so out of breath that his voice was a croak. "You are about the last thing I expected to meet on this planet!"

"*Maowrr?*" the cat inquired, pricking its ears forward and cocking its head to one side.

Tom slowly stretched a hand out to pet the animal, but it backed away and growled warningly.

"Sorry!" he apologized. "I didn't mean to scare you. How did you get here, anyway?"

The cat continued to eye him suspiciously.

"I saw you run into the passage with Ben and Ahn just before the doors closed," Tom said to the cat. "Now you're here. Therefore, there's got to be a connecting tunnel. Probably through that hole behind you. What do you think?"

The animal turned its head and licked its fur silently.

The young man sighed. "Well, excuse me. It

has been wonderful talking with you, but I have to find a way out of here!"

He began wiggling his way through the hole at the back of the ledge. The odor of dirt and mildew filled his nostrils as the rotted concrete-like material of the passage in front of him broke and crumbled around him.

The cat backed away from the opening uncertainly. Suddenly, it whirled around, away from the young inventor, and arched its back.

At that moment, Tom heard Ben scream!

"*Ben!*" the young inventor called as loudly as he could.

There was no answer.

As Tom strained to hear from his friend, the cat streaked past and disappeared into the darkness in front of him.

Tom began moving through the narrow tunnel once more.

Soon it grew so small that he was forced to crawl along on his stomach. Reaching in front of himself with his hands, he fought his way toward the place where he had heard Ben's scream.

His arms began to ache more than he could ever remember them aching before. It must be the gravity, he thought as sweat stung his eyes.

In spite of his determination to remain calm, he felt the beginnings of claustrophobia enveloping him. The tunnel roof seemed to press down on him, while his shoulders brushed the slimy walls of the passage.

"Think about space," he said to himself out loud. "Remember being in the spaceracer with Ben. Flying in all that vastness with nothing around you. Remember how big Jupiter looked from its moons."

Thump! His head cracked painfully against the roof when he tried to straighten up for some air.

Suddenly, he felt something wet around his ankles. Water!

The water in the main sewer chamber had risen to the level of the duct opening and was now flooding in. If it continued to rise, it would flood the duct and Tom would drown!

With the little bit of strength he had left, Tom increased his speed, reaching out blindly for handholds. His fingers were beginning to bleed, but he knew there was no way he could stop to rest.

The water was rapidly rising in the tiny tunnel. Although it was painful, Tom had to raise his chin to keep it out of the foul-smelling stream.

Then he heard a sound that charged him with hope—the gurgling sound of water drain-ing out of the tunnel. It was coming from somewhere in front of him. Tom laughed out loud with relief.

The sound grew louder with each few inches he moved forward. The darkness began to fade into gray. The end could not be far now.

Ahead of him, Tom saw the junction of three tunnels. The one he was crawling through went on and disappeared into darkness once again. To the right, a dark hole gaped. But to the left, Tom saw light. That must be where Ben is, Tom decided.

He took the left side of the junction and was relieved when it soon opened up into a larger duct.

"Ben!" he called out. His voice echoed down the dimly lit passage for a moment, then faded away altogether. There was no answer.

The tunnel was large enough for Tom to crawl on his hands and knees. He was moving along as quickly as he could without hurting himself on the rocky surface.

Then the young inventor saw the light grow brighter ahead of him. The tunnel was curving slightly and he decided that when he came to the end of the curve, he would be at the source of the light. The idea of reaching some kind of destination made him increase his speed.

Then he stopped in surprise. A few feet on the

other side of the turn, the tunnel ended abruptly!

Two heavy metal gates, meant to channel water from the duct to somewhere else, hung on rusty hinges. Some light shone into the passage on Tom's side from a small opening between the two gates. Tom's heart sank. Only a cat could get through a hole of that size!

A cat had, he thought ruefully. The dirty brown and black cat that had saved his life had led him here, and then abandoned him.

Ben must be on the other side of the gates!

Suddenly, a rasping sound came from behind him.

Tom turned and gasped, staring at the most horrible sight he had ever seen in his entire life!

Coming up slowly but steadily behind him was a thing he could only think of as half humanoid, half robot—a cyborg. A nightmare face with one glowing electronic eye stared at him. The face had an uneven smile that was due more to the creature's facial muscles than to any conscious expression of amusement.

The thing dragged itself through the tunnel jerkily, using one sharp, clawed mechanical arm to make progress. The other, a human arm, dragged limply at its side.

"Ahh . . . ahh . . . ahh," it grunted, creeping toward the young inventor.

Horrified, Tom grasped one of the gates by the small opening in the middle and tugged with all his strength.

It refused to budge!

"Ahh . . . ahh . . . ahhh," the cyborg cried behind him.

Tom backed up a few feet and ran at the metal gates, throwing his body against them.

A few grains of dirt fell from the top, but the gates did not move!

Tom felt a cold, metallic presence behind him and heard the sharp click of the creature's metal joints next to him.

"HELP!" he yelled, drawing out the word until his lungs ached.

Suddenly, a loud scraping noise made Tom look up. Two gigantic hooks with hydraulic joints grabbed the metal grates. He heard a loud grunt from beyond the barrier, then the material around it began to crumble. Metal groaned, bent, then broke.

Framed in the gaping hole was a massive humanoid encased in a metal exoskeleton. His arms terminated in hooks that still held the torn metal gates.

The humanoid tossed them aside as if they weighed nothing.

With horrified fascination, Tom watched the metal hooks reaching for him. "Tom Swift," the monster intoned. "I have been looking for you!"

Chapter Eight

Tom stared, mesmerized. "For me?" he managed to gasp. The cyborg behind him was cutting off his only escape route! Maybe he could outwit this monster.

"Are you sure you want *me*?" he asked.

Just then, Tom heard the soft thud of sneakers against stone and Ben's face suddenly popped into view.

"Tom! It's a good thing you yelled or we would never have known where you were!" the young Indian said, smiling. Then his face wrinkled in an involuntary expression of disgust. "Who's that behind you?"

In the relief of seeing Ben, Tom had momentarily forgotten about the cyborg behind him.

"That's Menge," the humanoid next to Ben rumbled in his deep voice. "He's really very nice. Aren't you, Menge?"

The ugly creature behind Tom bobbed up and down for a moment. Tom supposed that meant Menge was pleased, but it was awfully difficult to tell!

"I don't understand what this is all about," the young inventor said. "Could someone please clue me in?"

"Come with me," the massive humanoid said. "Oh, by the way, my name is Mataste. I'll explain everything soon."

Ben grinned at Tom and threw his arms over his friend's shoulders. "Let's go, buddy boy. There's food back at the ranch."

Suddenly, Tom realized those were the best words he had heard in a long time! "So what are we waiting for?" he asked happily.

Within a few minutes, they entered a vast cavern. Once part of the sewer system, it obviously had not been used for that purpose in years.

Tom stopped and gaped. All about him were dozens of cyborgs! He realized he was being impolite to stare so openly, but he could not help himself.

At a rough table on one side of the cavern, he

spotted Ahn talking with one of the cyborgs. Ahn did not seem pleased at the way the conversation was going.

Mataste handed Tom and Ben bowls of stew. Tom decided not to ask any questions about what kind of meat was in it.

Ben looked at him for a second. "Well," he said cautiously, "it smells terrific."

Tom took a couple of spoonfuls. "It's wonderful!" he exclaimed, as he ladled more of the stew into his mouth.

While the two boys gulped their food gratefully, Mataste settled himself on the floor next to Tom.

"Your friend here already knows something about us," he said, nodding toward Ben, "but I'll go through it again, anyway. All of us who live here in the sewers are victims of the robots."

Tom was horrified. "You mean, the robots conducted experiments on you and then let you go?" he asked.

"We escaped," Mataste corrected him. "We were once like Ahn and his people, but now we are part biologic and part robot. The villagers are terrified of us. Ahn is one of the few who will have anything to do with us and he must keep it secret. If his people knew he talked with us, they would shut him out of their community."

"But you were once one of them," Ben protested.

"Yes. But what people do not understand, they are afraid of," Mataste replied. "That is why we live here by ourselves." He gestured around him at the cavern.

"Someday we will be able to strike back at the robots. Until then, we wait and plan," he added.

"Don't the robots know about this place?" Tom asked.

"No," came the reply. "The robots never come into the sewers. They would rust too quickly. Since we are only partially robots, we are not bothered nearly as much."

"So you stay here and help Ahn's people sneak into the city?" Ben asked as he finished his stew.

"We do know quite a bit about the sewers and how to use them to get around. Unfortunately, almost all of the villagers are so afraid of us they would rather take their chances on the ground, with the robots," Mataste said sadly.

At that moment, Ahn came over to the two boys. "It'll be dark soon. We must leave now if we are to make it to the village by sunrise."

Tom would have liked to stay a little longer and talk with Mataste and the other cyborgs. Something was tugging at the back of his mind, but he was simply too tired to figure out what it was. But somehow the cyborgs seemed a key part of getting rid of the robots. Tom was sure of that.

"By the way," the young inventor said as he got slowly to his feet, "how can I get in touch with you? I think it only makes sense to work together against the robots."

Mataste was obviously moved. "Nothing would please us more!" he said. "There is an obscure entrance to the sewers on the outskirts of the city. It is at the very edge of the jungle. There always are two of us guarding that entrance. Go there and one of them will bring you to me."

He waved to one of the cyborgs, who approached the group.

"It is time for you to go," Mataste said. "Eino here will accompany you. We will meet again." Before Tom could reply, Mataste swiftly disappeared into one of the nearby tunnels.

Ahn and the cyborg led the boys into a huge duct on the other side of the cavern. On the way, Ben explained what had happened to him after the doors to the main sewer had closed.

"I tried to open the doors, even a little, so you could crawl through. But they are operated from some central place in the city. Anyway, Ahn knew that the cyborgs lived nearby."

"Is that why he was reluctant to go through the

sewers and then later to take the route we did?" Tom asked.

"I think so," Ben replied. "He realized the cyborgs would know how to rescue you, though. So we immediately headed to their cavern."

"But I heard you scream," Tom said.

"I screamed for the same reason you screamed, I'll bet!" the computer tech said. "We rounded a corner and there stood Mataste! He's a nice guy, but it's still pretty scary the first time you see him! Especially if you're not prepared for it!"

"I know exactly what you mean," Tom said ruefully.

"Say," Ben said suddenly. "How did you get all the way up by that set of gates? That was a long way from where we left you!"

"You won't believe it, but I followed a cat," Tom said.

"A cat?"

"A cat. A rather cute one at that," Tom explained.

"I suppose it was chasing a mouse and a dog was running after the cat," Ben suggested.

Tom shook his head in mock sorrow. "I told you you wouldn't believe me."

"Oh, Tom, be sensible. How could a cat get to this planet?" Ben demanded.

"Why does Ahn look very much like us? I'm sure a member of the Skree race might not even see any difference between us and Ahn," Tom suggested. "Why does the food we just ate taste so good to us? Remember how the Skree food tasted?"

"Please," Ben shuddered, "Don't remind me. I'd almost managed to forget that particular meal."

"Why are Ahn's facial expressions so similar to ours?" Tom continued.

"You have a point there," Ben agreed. "We can tell when he's angry or troubled or puzzled."

"All very human emotions," Tom put in.

"Yet he's an alien," Ben said slowly.

"But not as alien as the Skree," Tom pointed out.

Before Ben could reply, the small party halted. Eino turned to Tom. "Up ahead is the entrance of which Mataste spoke. I must stay here and guard it tonight. Have a safe journey."

Ahn held up his hand and told Tom and Ben, "Wait here just a moment."

He disappeared for a few minutes and then came running back. "Come!" he said to the boys.

They followed him down a short tunnel to a metal ladder which led to the open air.

"When you get to the top of the ladder, you

must not stop. It is very important that you immediately run after me into the jungle. Run straight ahead and do not stop for anything. We will meet at the foot of a large tree with red flowers. You cannot miss it. Any questions?"

Tom and Ben were puzzled, but shook their heads.

"Good. Let's go!" Ahn said. "Oh, one more thing. Good luck!"

Chapter Nine

First Ahn, then Ben, and finally Tom ran across the small clearing at the edge of the jungle and disappeared into the dense foliage.

Ahn was right. Just inside the jungle was a large tree with red flowers. When Tom arrived, Ahn told them what lay ahead of them.

"We will have to walk through the jungle all night. We will stop to rest only when we have to. We must get as far away from the city as we can while it is still night."

At Ben's puzzled look, he explained, "The robots used to come into the jungle only a short way. But recently they have been venturing deeper and deeper. They have also made machines which allow them to spend more time in the humid climate without rusting."

He shook his head sadly. "I don't want to take any chances. We must get to the village and warn my people about the chemical the robots are planning to use!"

As they followed Ahn, both Tom and Ben stared around them at the alien world. The trees seemed to have gigantic trunks. Most of them had brilliantly colored flowers several inches in diameter. All along the ground were green vines with tiny, delicate white blossoms.

Ahn seemed to know exactly where he was going, but if he was following a trail or a path, neither Ben nor Tom could see it. Yet Ahn picked his way purposefully around rocks and foliage.

They walked for hours. Ben and Tom could barely stay awake as they trudged on. The gravity of the planet made them feel as if they were carrying packs of thirty or forty pounds on their tired shoulders.

During the short rest stops, both boys fell instantly asleep. But far too soon, Ahn was shaking them awake.

Once, Tom paused beneath one of the huge trees. He estimated it would take at least seven people joining hands to encircle it. And that was not even the largest tree he had seen in the jungle.

The branches hung down, forming a leafy green veil. Some dragged on the ground and their tips seemed to merge with the branches of the other trees. The perfume of the flowers was strong and almost sickeningly sweet.

Tom would have liked to have rested under the tree, but back in the city, Anita and Aristotle were prisoners of the robots. He knew he had to reach Ahn's village in order to free his friends. In his tired mind, the young inventor was still trying to come up with a plan to help the humanoids defeat the mechanical monsters. He wished there was some way to find out more of the history of the planet and what had gone wrong between Ahn's people and the robots.

"Are you okay, Tom?" Ben asked.

"Sure." Tom smiled wearily. "Just thinking," he added as he trudged on once again.

Suddenly, Ahn stopped and gestured for the boys to do the same.

"What—" Tom began, but the humanoid motioned him to be silent.

They stood still, listening to the sounds of the jungle.

Ben turned to Tom and mouthed the words, "I don't hear anything."

Tom shrugged.

"I think we're being followed," Ahn whispered, coming closer to the boys. "I've had that feeling ever since we left the city."

"We're all tired," Tom said. "Let's keep going. Ben and I will keep our ears open, too. If we hear anything unusual, we'll signal you."

Ahn nodded in agreement and they resumed their walking.

It was dawn. Already, the air was heating up under the canopy of leaves and branches formed by the giant trees.

A short distance ahead, Ahn stopped again to listen. This time, Tom heard something, too. Behind them, leaves rustled for a moment, then there was silence in the jungle once more.

Tom caught Ben's attention and raised his eyebrows in warning. He searched the dense foliage around them, but could not see anything.

Then he heard another rustle of leaves. A sudden rush of adrenaline brought him to full alertness. It was the fear of an invisible enemy that might be lurking nearby. After the horrors he had encountered in the city, Tom was prepared for just about anything.

Ahn and the boys crouched in fighting positions. Tom tensed his muscles expectantly. His hands twitched with excitement.

It seemed as if all animal and insect sounds in the jungle had stopped! The air was still.

"Maowrr!" came a small growl from underneath a bush next to Tom.

"What?" the young inventor exclaimed.

"Maowrr," came the answer.

The dirty brown and black cat marched out of the underbrush. It stepped in front of Tom and looked up at him fearlessly. *"Maowrr!"* it stated firmly.

"That's a cat!" Ben cried. "It really is an Earth-type cat! You weren't kidding me!"

Tom reached down to pet the animal, but it backed away. It did not run, but stood looking at him just out of reach.

"He wants friendship, but on his own terms!" Ben laughed. "I suppose cats are the same all over the galaxy."

"I don't know why the two of you are so excited about a common *wakka,*" Ahn said. "We have them in the village. They do a good job of keeping the vermin away."

He turned and began walking briskly through the jungle once again. "We're wasting our time," he called over his shoulder.

"Sorry if it sounds like we've gone crazy or something, but we also have these animals on our planet, Earth!" Ben said.

Ahn seemed genuinely interested in that. "As far as I know, *wakkas* have always lived among us. There is someone in the village you must talk to. He will be interested to hear of your *wakkas*."

As they walked on, Tom glanced behind him. The cat was following at a respectable distance, stopping occasionally to investigate a suspicious root, or smell an insect.

"You're just as dirty as I am," Tom called to the cat. "This sure beats the sewer, eh, fella? What's your name, anyway? You never told me last time we talked."

"Uh-oh! Cute animal alert! Cute animal alert!" Ben called out. "Once you name them, you know it's hard to get rid of them! Where we're going we don't have time to keep track of a pet. Who knows what we'll be up against?"

Ben watched the cat stay just far enough behind the boys to keep them in sight. "He is interesting-looking, though. See how his chin is darker than the rest of him? It almost looks like he has a beard."

"Put a cigar in his mouth and he'd look like General Ulysses Grant," said Tom. "He even acts like a general. Besides, I'm not bringing him along. He's coming with us and we don't have anything to say about it."

"A typical cat," Ben retorted and both boys started to laugh.

Their amusement was cut short by a strange noise in the distance.

Tom could not identify what it was, but it sounded like trees crashing!

The cat pricked its ears forward, listening. Then, suddenly, it raced for a nearby tree and climbed it with lightning speed.

"We should do the same thing," the young inventor said to Ahn, pointing to the cat. It was now perched on a sturdy branch halfway up the huge tree. "We'd be able to get an aerial view of whatever it is that's causing all the fuss."

Ben and Ahn boosted Tom up until he could grab the bottom branch. He held on to a ropelike section of a hanging vine and helped Ben and Ahn up. After that, it was easy to climb from limb to limb, since the branches were close together.

Finally, Tom crawled out as far as he could and peered into the distance. He saw a massive shape moving slowly but steadily toward them. Around it, branches and vines were being thrown high into the air. The thing was clearing a path ahead of itself!

Tom squinted. He could hear what seemed to

be the sound of metal joints creaking. It blended with the noise of crashing and ripping through the jungle. He remembered old adventure movies he had seen about herds of elephants crashing through jungles on Earth.

"It's some kind of machine," he called out at last. "It's throwing branches and leaves—hey, what's the matter?"

Ahn had moved toward Tom on the branch. As he looked at the source of the noise, his face turned white with fear.

When Ahn did not answer Tom's question, the young man turned back to watch the progress of the thing. The massive dark metal shape was like a steamroller. With a sudden jolt, Tom realized that it was not merely throwing branches. It was uprooting entire gigantic trees and tossing them hundreds of feet into the air!

Then Ahn uttered one word, his voice choked with fear.

The TTUs translated it as *berserker*.

Chapter Ten

"If we stay in this tree, we'll be sitting ducks!" Tom shouted. "It's coming this way!"

"If we get down on the ground, we'll be *squashed* ducks!" Ben yelled in return. "We'll never be able to run fast enough to get out of its way!"

"It's coming from the direction of my village," Ahn wailed. "For all I know, it may have destroyed my home and family!"

Tom took a last look at the horror that was bearing down on them all too fast.

"What's the plan, Tom?" Ben asked.

98   "We're going to punt," Tom responded.

"What does that mean?" Ahn asked, his bushy eyebrows knitted together in a frown.

"He's thinking," Ben replied.

The ground was shaking and Tom, Ben, and Ahn could feel the vibrations up in the tree.

"Where's General Grant?" Ben asked anxiously.

"Who?" Tom asked.

"The cat. You said he looked like General Grant," his friend answered.

"If he's smart, he's long gone!" Tom grumbled.

"*Maowrr?*" came a voice nearby.

"If we were smart, *we'd* be gone," said Ben.

"I want to examine this robot," said Tom. "Let's stay here and play with it a little while!"

"Have you lost your mind?" Ben cried. "That thing is liable to tear us to pieces and, frankly, I'm fond of all my pieces!"

"Don't you see my point?" the young inventor asked. "We haven't had the opportunity to find out about the robot technology on this planet. We don't know what we're up against. Who was it that said, 'Know your enemy'?"

"Probably General Grant," Ben suggested.

"*Maowrr!*" the cat commented.

"See, he agrees with me!" Tom chuckled. Then he became serious again. "The robots are planning to destroy all biological life on this planet and we don't know how to stop them, how to use their own weaknesses to defeat them!"

"I think I understand your point," Ahn said. "Still, 'playing' with a berserker is a frightening thought."

"Don't get the wrong idea. I'm plenty scared!" Tom said. "I guess the vote is three to one, huh?"

"General Grant can't vote!" Ben said.

Tom grinned. "Are you going to tell him?"

They could see the huge robot in the center of the path it was clearing for itself through the jungle growth. Tom admitted it was a dramatic sight.

"It looks like one of those old military land tanks with arms," Ben commented.

"That's an oversimplification, but I see what you mean," Tom agreed. He winced at the crackling, mushing sound of the jungle being crushed under the thing's treads. "It doesn't have much maneuverability, does it?" he asked.

"Berserkers usually move in a straight line. But occasionally they do not," said Ahn.

"Tom, look! A scythe!" Ben exclaimed.

"You're right! One arm slices through the plant and the other, the three-fingered waldo, picks it up and tosses it into the back storage bin,"

Tom said. He watched it thoughtfully for a moment.

"The berserkers must have been built originally as some kind of harvester or land-clearing equipment," the young inventor added.

"It's partially fulfilling its programing," Ben pointed out. "See, it's tossing the trees and plants into the air, but only some of them are filling up the bin in back. I wonder what it does when the bin is full. It must have an automatic dump cycle."

"Ben, give me your key ring. Quickly!" Tom ordered.

"Here." Ben handed it to his friend with a puzzled look on his face. "What are you going to do? Wait until it gets to our tree and jump on it? I don't think any of our keys will fit its ignition system—just in case you were thinking of trying to drive it away."

"No, I don't plan to jump on it. But you're close." Tom said. He stared intently as the giant robot moved ever closer to the boys.

"Uh-oh! Here we go!" called Ben.

At that moment, the brown and black cat made a mighty leap, landing with all four feet on the ground. The approaching robot stopped still, its sensors swinging from the tree to the cat.

"Looks like General Grant has decided to duck out of this campaign," Tom said. "I think we should follow suit. Come on!" he yelled and began to scramble down the huge tree.

Seconds after the boys reached the ground, the huge robot shifted its attention from the path the cat had taken back to the tree. It reached out with its hooks and sank them effortlessly into rough bark.

"Stay absolutely still!" Tom called to his friends. Mystified, they obeyed.

Just then, the cat streaked across the path of the robot, darting from the bushes toward the young men. The berserker withdrew its hooks from the tree and swung them in the direction of the cat. The furry animal scrambled into the underbrush.

As a sensor glided past the immobile Tom Swift, he suddenly hurled Ben's key ring as hard as he could. It flew through the air, striking the front of the sensor exactly in the middle. The sound of shattering glass was followed by a puff of smoke.

The sensor dangled uselessly! It was dead!

Tom took careful aim at another sensor and threw his own key ring at it. Again, glass broke and a shower of sparks indicated that a second sensor was out of commission.

"Got you!" Ben cried gleefully. He picked up a sizable rock from the ground and ruined a third sensor.

Ahn watched, openmouthed with amazement, as the two boys worked on deactivating the berserker.

With almost all of its sensors nonfunctional, the giant robot turned slowly in circles for a few minutes. Then it simply stood still.

"You've done it!" Ahn exclaimed. "You killed a berserker!"

"Not really," Tom quickly corrected him. "It's still very much alive, but with its sensors out, it has no idea where to go."

Seeing the puzzled look on Ahn's face, Ben explained further. "The berserker can only do what it is told to do. This machine was told to clear land. Since it can no longer see what to clear, it simply stopped."

"All we did was damage the berserker's 'eyes'— its sensors," Tom summed up.

"It's magic!" Ahn said with awe.

"Not magic!" Tom said sternly. "It was only common sense with a little ingenuity. Plus some knowledge of how robots work," he added.

"Now what?" asked Ben.

"How far is the village from here?" Tom asked the alien.

"Only an hour or so away," Ahn replied.

"As much as I would like to investigate this robot, I think we should get going. Perhaps we'll find some useful information there," Tom said. "Besides, I'm simply too tired to do a good job examining the berserker carefully."

"Aren't you afraid the other robots will come and get this thing?" Ben asked.

"There's always that possibility. But we have to chance it," Tom said, studying the berserker intently.

Finally, he spoke again. "Ben, does that metal look familiar to you?" he asked.

The computer tech cautiously approached the stilled robot and peered at it closely. "Hey, am I seeing things? This seems remarkably like the alloy we used to cover the *Exedra* just before leaving Swift Enterprises a few days ago!"

"That's what I thought," Tom said. "There's no way to be sure without taking part of it to the lab, but it makes sense."

"It does? How?" the young computer tech asked.

"Consider: a race of people arrive on this planet to colonize it. What's the very first thing they do?"

"Provide temporary shelter for themselves," Ben responded.

"Okay. What's the second thing they do?"

"Make some kind of permanent homes." Suddenly Ben's face lit up with excitement. "Of course! To build houses in a jungle you have to clear a lot of land!"

"You've got it! If the spaceship that brought you here is not able to take you away for some reason, you use its outer hull to build a giant land-clearing machine!" Tom grinned.

"There would be no problems with rust. It would be strong—"

"And who knows what other advantages it might have?" Tom finished for his friend. "If we are correct, it means the berserkers and its brothers were already working before the robots took over. There's a good possibility it is not connected to the Unimind—at least, not the same way the robots built by other robots are tied in. That might buy us some time."

Ahn had been following the discussion avidly. His face reflected his excitement. "Are you sure?" he blurted out. "Did the Old Ones really build this machine?"

"I think we'll know for sure before too long," Tom said. "But it seems consistent with what Aristotle told us and what little we've observed so far. Now we just have to figure out how to use this knowledge to our benefit and against the robots." He grinned at Ahn tiredly. "In the meantime, let's get to your village."

"You must see Teo," Ahn said solemnly. "He will aid you." Without explaining further, the young alien once again began marching through the jungle.

The small party stopped in the middle of a giant gourd cluster. The gourds hung to the ground, their great weight bending the tree branches to which they were attached. Tom wondered if Ahn had made a wrong turn somewhere.

Suddenly—from out of the gourds—came people! The boys were surrounded instantly!

Chapter Eleven

Ahn grinned at the boys. "Welcome to my home," he said.

Tom laughed. He had expected the village to be made of huts. But what could be more natural than to use the hollowed-out gourds for housing?

He noticed that the leaves and vines above the village were just a little more densely woven together than nature had intended. Terrific camouflage, he said to himself.

"These are my friends," Ahn told the people gathered around the boys. "Without them, I never could have escaped the city."

"Where are the others?" one woman asked.

Ahn shook his head sadly. "I'm sorry. The Metal Ones took them away."

Quickly, Ahn told the people of the robots' newest plan to use a chemical which would destroy all biological life on the planet. He also recounted the experience the boys had just had with the berserker.

"But how can that be?" one woman asked. "To kill a berserker is impossible."

"I quite agree," Tom said. "It's not dead, merely stopped for a while. But the most important thing is to deal with the robots and their new threat."

"Come," Ahn said to the boys. "You must meet Teo. He will have some ideas."

The boys walked to one of the largest gourd-huts. Outside, sitting in the shade, was a very old man. Ahn introduced the boys.

"This is Teo," he said to Tom and Ben. "He knows all of the stories about the Old Ones."

Quickly, Ahn retold his adventures since leaving the village several days before. In this account, unlike his earlier one to the villagers, Ahn included the happenings with the cyborgs in the sewers.

"But the strangest event of all was a Metal One who helped us to escape," Ahn finished. "He was made by Tom and is friendly with Tom and Ben's people!"

"Once that was true here, also," Teo said softly.

"Aristotle said your people were known as the Karshe—" Tom began. He stopped when he saw the expression on the face of the two aliens.

"I'm sorry, did I say something wrong?" he asked. The young inventor suddenly remembered that Ahn had reacted strongly when Aristotle had mentioned that bit of news.

"No," Teo replied. "There is no way for you to know. That is the holiest of our old words. It is used only during ceremonies that are held seven times a year. To utter it at other times is considered a great wrong."

"I'm sorry," Tom said hastily. "I meant no disrespect."

"Please," Teo urged. "Continue what you were saying. What else did your Metal One tell you of our past?"

"Not much," Tom admitted. "There was very little time. He was helping us to escape from the robots. He only commented that the robots who now control the city are not as complex as he is."

"He also said Ahn's people built the city," Ben added. "The building where we were held was originally used as a science complex."

Ahn and Teo again looked startled.

"Oh, dear," Ben said. "Did I accidentally say one of your holy words?"

"Yes," Teo said slowly. " 'Science' is considered almost as holy as 'Karshe.' "

Teo sat silently for several minutes. He rocked slowly back and forth, gazing up at the top of the trees. Finally, he struggled to his feet and disappeared inside the gourd-hut.

Ben and Tom looked at each other in puzzlement. Before they could say anything, Ahn gestured for the two of them to remain quiet. Teo returned with a square box. It was made of black plastic and was about two feet square.

Ahn glanced around nervously when he saw what Teo was carrying.

"This is the holiest of our holy things. It is supposed to be opened only during one of the seven ceremonies I mentioned. Inside is all that we have from our forebears," Teo explained.

He carefully placed the box on the ground and knelt beside it. "If what I am doing is wrong, I pray forgiveness. But perhaps what is inside can help us in the fight against the Metal Ones."

He paused for a moment, then slowly lifted the cover of the box. Tom and Ben leaned over to see what was inside.

"Ben, look!" Tom exclaimed.

"Can these help?" Teo asked anxiously.

"May we examine them closely?" Tom asked.

"Of course. Here," the elderly man said, reaching inside for the two objects.

"What do you call them on your world?" Ahn asked.

"I'm not sure," Tom said. "I think this must be a computer of some sort." He pointed to a small, square metal object with rows of buttons and a blank screen.

"Probably," Ben agreed. "Hard to say until we poke around in it." He turned his attention to the second object. "This seems to be a radio or walkie-talkie."

"And there's the aerial," Tom added, pointing to a long, slender wire on the top of the object.

"Here," Teo said. He handed the boys several plastic cards. They were filled with diagrams and writing in an unfamiliar language.

"These are the oldest objects we have," Teo explained. "Stories say our forefathers used these when they lived in the city."

Tom frowned thoughtfully. "What do the stories tell you about your ancestors? Do they tell where they came from?"

Teo nodded. "Stories say that they came from

the stars and that they brought the Metal Ones with them. At first the Metal Ones helped the people, but then there was trouble."

"How did the robots take over?" Tom asked.

"No one knows," Teo sighed. "There is much the stories do not tell."

He looked at the two boys anxiously. "Will these things help you fight the Metal Ones?" he asked.

"We can't tell for sure yet," Tom replied. "But I expect they'll at least give us some clues. Do you understand any of the writing on the cards?" he asked.

"A few words," Teo said. "But it is impossible to tell what it all means."

"The cards are schematic designs of some kind," Ben said.

For the first time in several minutes, Ahn spoke. "Teo, my friends and I are very tired. Perhaps they could sleep here with you. That way they will be close to the holy objects."

"That will be fine. Come with me," Teo said as he replaced the computer, the radio, and the cards in the black box.

The boys followed him into the gourd-hut. To Tom's surprise, except for the odd, organic shape of the room, there was no way to tell they were inside a plant. Teo placed blankets on two pallets on the floor.

"You may sleep here," he said.

Tom thanked the man and stretched out. He tried to remember what the radio or walkie-talkie looked like, but he was asleep before he could even picture them in his mind.

When he woke up several hours later, he was all alone. Rubbing his eyes, the young inventor stumbled outside where it was still daylight. Ben was squatting in the middle of dozens of mechanical parts, happily eating a piece of fruit.

"There you are," the computer tech greeted him. "I thought you were going to sleep all day. Try some of this fruit. It's delicious."

Tom took the fruit. "Hmm. It *is* good. A cross between a plum and an orange," Tom said between juicy mouthfuls. "Why aren't you sleeping?" he asked his friend.

"I was too excited to rest more than a couple of hours," Ben explained. "Teo and I have been taking the computer and radio apart. Only the radio isn't a radio. It's a remote-control device."

"Maybe it was used to control robots," Tom suggested.

"Perhaps," Ben agreed. "Right now we're recharging the solar batteries. Both devices used solar energy."

"I'm going back to examine the berserker," Tom declared. "I hope I'm ahead of the robots. Being able to go over that massive machine would be a big help for us."

"Wait a couple of minutes and I'll go with you." Ben began reassembling the remote-control device. "It'll give me a chance to test this thing."

He was just about finished when Ahn walked up. The boys told him they were going to check out the berserker and he quickly volunteered to come with them.

An hour later, the three approached the stilled berserker. Tom motioned the other two closer to him.

"We have to be careful from here on. It's possible the robots have discovered their harvester isn't working. Perhaps they have come up to check on it, and we don't want to barge into a group of them."

Ahn and Ben nodded. "We should stay under cover as much as possible. Let me go first," Ahn suggested.

Moving from behind trees and bushes, the small group cautiously approached the area the berserker had cleared before being stopped by Tom and Ben.

"I don't see anything," Ben whispered.

"It seems deserted enough," Tom agreed. "And I doubt the robots would think of hiding and ambushing us. Besides, they probably don't even know we're here. It looks safe to me."

The boys quickly ran over to the robot. Ahn moved much more cautiously, still afraid the berserker would suddenly spring back to life.

Ben thoughtfully tapped the side of the mechanoid. "I'd love to run a test on a sample of this stuff," he said, his fingers tracing a pattern on the metal. "I wish we had the lab from the *Exedra* here."

"Speaking of the *Exedra,* I hope the robots have not been able to find a way to bypass the hatch locks!" Tom said.

"That's all we need!" Ben muttered, concern in his voice. "Imagine what they would do if they managed to dig through the computer and locate the coordinates of Earth and the Sol system! After all, why destroy biological life on only one planet?"

Tom shook his head gravely. "Just one more reason why we have to stop them—and fast!" he said.

"Listen!" Ahn said suddenly.

They stopped and strained their ears. A faint whirring noise was coming from somewhere above them. Tom could not identify it, but it sounded like a helicopter. Could it be a robot chopper? he wondered.

Just then a dark shadow appeared over the tops of the trees at the edge of the clearing.

"A flying Metal One!" Ahn exclaimed.

Chapter Twelve

Tom could see the fear on the face of his humanoid friend.

"We don't have time to make it to the jungle," Ben called out.

"This way!" Tom said as he ran to the back of the berserker. He dived through an opening and into the storage bin of the mechanical harvester. Ben followed right behind him, but Ahn stopped just outside the door. The humanoid was shaking with fright.

"I—I can't," he cried. "Inside a berserker, no!" He shook his head rapidly.

"Quickly!" Tom ordered sternly. "You have no other choice."

Ben simply reached out and grabbed Ahn's right arm. Tom took the left one and the two boys hauled the shaking alien into the bin.

No sooner had they burrowed beneath the tree branches than they heard the sound of whirling blades overhead.

Evidently, the chopper was hovering, trying to decide whether the berserker required further study. The noise of the blades stayed directly above them for several minutes. Tom could hardly resist the strong temptation to look at the flying mechanoid.

Minutes passed. The spy robot had not changed its position. Tom wondered what it could be studying so intently.

Finally, the young inventor moved so he could peer out of the door to the bin. A short distance away, he could see the distinct form of the dirty brown and black cat!

The animal was sitting with its ears pointed in Tom's direction. It was obviously trying to decide whether to join the boys in the bin or stay where it was.

Tom hoped the cat would stay where it was. Apparently, it was the reason why the spy robot was hovering above them. It had been programed to be curious about anything living.

"It's General Grant!" Tom whispered to Ben.

"The reconnaissance robot is studying him."

"I'm grateful for all the times that cat has helped us out, but now his loyalty could get us killed!" Ben muttered.

The cat took a few tentative steps toward them. Its head stretched forward, sniffing the familiar scent of Tom, Ben, and Ahn.

"Go away! Go away!" Tom hissed softly.

The cat stopped to lick its fur.

Ben moaned. "What a time for a bath!"

"Cats always do that when they're undecided or feeling insecure," said Tom. "It's what he'll do when he makes up his mind that bothers me!"

Suddenly, a white-hot bolt of flame spewed from the hovering robot. Only the sewer-born cat's lightning reflexes saved it. The animal jumped high into the air above and landed on all four feet. The instant it was on the ground again, General Grant streaked straight for the storage bin.

"The game's over," shouted Tom. "We can't let the robot get back to base."

All at once, the cat skidded to a stop, then leaped to the left of the opening. Another tongue of flame shot out.

"Uh-oh. What's this?" Ben asked.

Tom looked to where his friend was pointing. There was a small puddle of liquid forming on the floor by the opening. The young inventor bent down, dipped his fingers into the fluid, and smelled them.

"Hydraulic fluid!" he declared. "The berserker must be damaged somehow."

Ben groaned. "That's all we need. A puddle of hydraulic fluid near us and the flying robot shooting flame all over the place!"

Just then, the cat hurled itself into the storage bin. It was followed by another burst of flame, which hit the pool of fluid by the door. A giant explosion lit up the inside of the berserker! Tom knew the flames would quickly envelop the entire storage bin. The branches and other foliage would burn quickly.

Already, dirty black smoke was billowing thickly, filling everyone's lungs!

Desperately, Tom looked around. On the opposite side of the bin was a second door.

"This way!" he shouted.

Ben and Ahn followed as Tom wiggled and climbed his way through the tree limbs.

"Hurry!" Ben shouted. "The fire's gaining on us!"

The trio raced through the door, only seconds before the entire inside of the bin burst into flame.

Tom glanced up into the sky. The spy robot

was globe-shaped. Sensors and other probing equipment protruded from the surface. Long, spindly legs with special shock-absorbing sockets hung limply, just inches above the ground.

"Now what?" Ben asked.

"Now's the time to try your remote-control device," Tom replied.

"But I don't know how it works. I'm not even certain it *is* a remote-control device," Ben countered.

"It's our only hope," Tom said as he reached for the metal object. "Stay still. If we run, the chopper will start throwing flame again."

He pointed the antenna directly at the helicopter robot. There were seven buttons and a knob on the device. With no way to know what any of them were for, the young inventor simply pushed the buttons one after another.

"Nothing's happening!" Ben cried.

"At least the thing stopped shooting," Tom commented. "But as soon as it finishes whatever tests it is now running on us, it will probably start with the flame again."

Suddenly, the device in Tom's hand began to hum. "Well, it's turned on," Tom said.

"So make it do something," Ben said.

"Be glad to, ol' buddy, but I just ran out of buttons!" Tom answered.

He looked up at the spy robot. Its helicopter blades still whirred. Nothing seemed to have changed. Desperately, Tom twisted a knob on the side of the device toward him.

The helicopter suddenly zoomed several feet into the sky!

"Tom!" Ben cried.

"So that's how this thing works!" Tom grinned at his friend.

A tongue of flame narrowly missed the boys.

"You've made it mad!" Ben said.

"A robot with emotions?" Tom asked. "I doubt it." He twisted the knob away from himself as far as it would go.

To their amazement. the robot helicopter plummeted toward the ground! It dropped into the burning storage bin with a tremendous crash. Seconds later, an enormous explosion knocked the boys off their feet.

Tom picked himself up off the ground. "Wow! That was something!"

"This will surely bring the other robots," Ahn said, concerned.

Tom nodded. "We'll have to be somewhere else when they arrive."

"I don't understand," Ben complained.

"The storage bin probably detaches from the main part of the berserker," Tom explained. "As soon as it's cool enough to get a bit closer, we'll check."

"But what are we going to do with a berserker?" Ben asked. "We can hardly drive it into the city and knock down the buildings until we find Anita and Aristotle."

"You're right. But you're not far from what I plan to do. We're going to use the berserker as our headquarters while we get ourselves an army," Tom explained.

"An army?" Ben asked, his eyebrows raised.

"Right. First you start with one berserker, then you add a few stray robots," Tom said.

Before Ben could reply, the black and brown cat stalked over to the small group. It marched straight to Tom and began to rub itself against his ankles, purring loudly.

Tom laughed. "That's a switch. General Grant must have decided we're okay after all." He bent down and picked the cat up. It continued to purr.

"Want to come hunt robots with us, General?" the young inventor asked.

The cat put his nose to Tom's face, looked hesitant, then said, "*Maowrr*."

"I guess that settles it." Ben chuckled.

"Time to go to work, General," Tom said as he put the cat back on the ground.

The boys walked over to the berserker, standing as close to the still-burning storage bin as they could.

"See," Tom pointed above them, "it's attached by those couplers. The bin and the berserker both have metal circles on one end. The circles are lined up with each other and a rod is slipped through them."

"So all we have to do is push the rod out and drive the berserker away," Ben finished.

"You've got it. We can use tree branches to push the rods out," Tom said.

Within a few minutes, the storage bin had been disconnected.

"Now we have to get into the robot and figure out how to move it," Tom said.

Ahn's face turned white, but he said nothing.

"How do you propose we do that?" Ben asked.

"There must be a way into the thing. Some kind of access for repairs, if nothing else," the young inventor replied.

The boys walked around the berserker, examining it carefully.

"Here we go!" Ben called from the other side. Tom and Ahn ran over to him. The computer tech opened a door and stepped into the harvester.

A few feet beyond the door was a ladder which

stretched upward. All around them were the
exposed gears and machinery which drove the
robot.

"We must be right in the center of the engine,"
Tom observed.

Ben pointed to the ladder. "Do we?" he asked.

"We'll have to, eventually, so we might as well
now," Tom said. "I'll go first."

Quickly he climbed to the top of the ladder
and entered a small room. "Hey, we're in luck!"
he called back.

Ben and Ahn swiftly joined him.

Ahn's face reflected the battle going on inside
him. Part of him was still very much afraid of the
berserker. But part of him was filled with awe to
be doing something none of his people had done
for generations.

Ben looked around the small room in which
they found themselves. "Wow!" he exclaimed.
"This is something!"

Chapter Thirteen

"This robot was obviously built to be run by Ahn's people, as well as to function on its own," Tom said.

"You're right. We *are* in luck!" Ben exclaimed. "Now all we have to do is to figure out how it all works!"

Tom and Ben studied the controls carefully.

"The first thing we have to do is to disconnect the berserker from the rest of the robots. Any idea how we do that?" Tom asked.

"Well, that's obviously the computer," Ben said, pointing to the center of the control panel. "It looks very much like the one in the black box back in the village."

He hesitantly made a few entries on the computer keyboard. "It seems to be fairly standard, even though it's a bit different from what I'm used to. Until I check it all out thoroughly, I wouldn't want to have to do anything fancy."

"Pulling it from the robots' hookup shouldn't be too fancy, should it?" Tom asked.

"No. But it will take a while. And until I find the correct sequence, the robots will know something funny is going on here," Ben said.

"Well, we can't help that," Tom sighed. "Why don't you just go straight to the memory banks and ask it to display the different guidance systems? That way we won't waste time."

"I could do that," Ben agreed. "But if the robots had any smarts at all, they'd know exactly what we're up to."

"If they have any smarts at all, they will know what we're up to before very long, anyway. So let's disconnect the berserker sooner rather than later," Tom pointed out.

"Smart thinking, chief," Ben saluted his friend. "This'll take a bit of time, so make yourself comfortable." The young Indian paused for a minute, then began tapping away on the keyboard, his face a mask of concentration.

Tom's eyes wandered over the rest of the control panel. All at once they lit up. "Hey, Ben, a radio!" he exclaimed. "And that must be a microphone!"

It was. It took Tom only a few minutes of slight modifications to adjust the radio controls to Aristotle's channel.

"How are you coming, Ben?" he asked.

"I think I've got it," his friend replied. "I want to put in some kind of blocking shield. It will be primitive, but at least we'll have some warning before the robots try and recapture the berserker's computer."

Tom began to broadcast on Aristotle's channel.

"Tom, is that really you?" his mechanoid asked. *"Your voice sounds choked up. Is that what they call human emotion?"*

"Yes." Tom laughed. "Tell me, what's happening there?"

"Anita is in great danger, I am sorry to report," the robot said.

Tom's heart sank, as he and Ben exchanged worried looks.

"I am a prisoner, although they have a more polite way of phrasing it. I am confined to a small laboratory where I am requested to experiment on some portions of the robots which have developed malfunctions," Aristotle went on.

"Doctor Aristotle!" Tom joked. "How are your patients?"

"My patients are very good. Unfortunately, Anita is about to become a patient of the robots."

"What do you mean?" Tom asked anxiously.

"As you know, her brain and nervous system order her leg. The robots are trying to reprogram her on-board computer to direct her organic brain," Aristotle explained.

Both Tom and Ben winced.

"In other words, instead of her artificial leg being a part of her, the robots are trying to make her a part of the leg," Tom exclaimed. With a shudder, he thought of the cyborg horrors they had seen in the sewers.

"Yes. You are correct. I am stalling for time. The robots are using me for some of their finer calibrations. I can partially mislead them by sending them on incorrect paths, but I dare not do it too frequently."

"Got it!" Ben exclaimed. He flashed Tom the thumbs-up sign.

"Aristotle, are you being monitored?" Tom asked. He knew the robot was not capable of lying to him.

"Not on this channel," came the reply. *"I have managed to keep this part of me secret from the robots. They seem content, although somewhat suspicious, as long as they have access to the rest of me. They are not positive there is a part of me which they do not know."*

Having been assured the conversation was

secret from the Unimind, Tom told Aristotle about the objects in the box back in the village.

"Very interesting," Aristotle replied. *"From the way you describe the computer, it must be the A-282 model about which I have been reading so much in the library here. Those cards with the diagrams slide right into the back of the device."*

"You mean like the old-fashioned keypunch cards?" Ben asked.

"Somewhat along the same principle. Only these cards contained thousands of complex programs. One thing I will happily say for the Karshe is they were quite adept at the science of miniaturization. Those cards could contain the knowledge from dozens of libraries."

Ben whistled softly through his teeth. "Seems like that's quite a find."

"Whether your people knew it consciously or not, they were saving the very part of their past which would reconnect them with it," Tom said to Ahn.

The alien nodded silently.

"Forgive me, Tom. I do not even know how you are broadcasting to me. I believe the humanoids on this planet are rather unsophisticated scientifically. It seems unlikely, based on my reading, that they would have a radio capable of broadcasting on this narrow frequency," Aristotle commented.

Tom quickly filled the mechanoid in on what

had happened. When he explained about stopping the berserker and causing the spy robot to crash, Aristotle interrupted him excitedly.

"Now I understand much more what the robots are doing. Be careful. You are in danger by remaining where you are!"

Tom and Ben exchanged looks of concern.

"The loss of two robots within such a short period of time has drawn their attention to that section. However, they have not, of course, yet connected the losses with you or Ben. And they know the Karshe are incapable of such technical feats. So the robots are more curious than angry. They are planning to send out a rather large group to explore the area," Aristotle said.

Suddenly, Ahn spoke. "There is a huge field where the Metal Ones go and stay. Never has a Metal One left it, once it goes there."

Tom and Ben looked at the young alien in surprise.

"Perhaps the berserker could go there and hide from the Metal Ones who are searching for it," Ahn suggested.

"Boy, you have the makings of a good military tactician!" Ben exclaimed, both surprised and delighted.

"Aristotle, does the library have records on such a place?" Tom asked.

"Yes. There is a large collection of earth-clearing

machines. They were driven to the spot and then turned off and abandoned. This was many generations ago. The robots have not had any dealing with them since," came the reply.

"But why would they simply abandon some of their own kind?" Ben asked.

"Once they took over, they decided to do away with all biological life on this planet," Aristotle explained. *"Clearing the land was a priority of the Karshe, but it meant nothing to robots. So the mechanoids that had been engaged in that activity were simply abandoned."*

"But why didn't the robots try to change their programing?" Ben asked. "It seems like a waste to simply let all that material sit unused."

"The Unimind calculated it would be easier to build new robots specifically constructed to its needs than to rebuild the existing ones," Aristotle reported.

Tom turned to Ahn. "Can you guide us to this abandoned field?" he asked.

"Yes. It is forbidden for my people to go there, but I do know where it is," he replied.

"Good. Ben, have you figured out how to drive this thing yet?" Tom asked.

"I think I've got it," the young Indian responded.

The radio crackled as Aristotle once again spoke. *"Tom, it would be wise for you to leave the vicinity as soon as possible. I have been monitoring as much of the robots' communications as I can. Two rather distressing pieces of information just entered my memory banks."*

"Out with it, Aristotle," Tom exclaimed.

"One is that the exploration force has just left the city to investigate the out-of-commission robots. They should arrive within a few hours, as they are moving quite rapidly."

"What's the other news?" Tom asked Aristotle anxiously.

"It is about Anita."

Tom and Ben exchanged concerned glances. They were upset that they were not able to be with the redhead. Though they realized that they were in a better position to help her as long as they were not within the power of the robots, both boys felt guilty that their friend was a prisoner while they were not.

"The robots are preparing Anita for the operation now," Aristotle went on.

Tom's heart sank. They had so much to do! How could they even get to her before it was too late?

"Okay, Aristotle. Thanks for the news," Tom said. "We're moving out of here. I'm going to rig the berserker to continue to monitor this wavelength. We've done all right so far, but I don't want to press our luck by talking with you any more than absolutely necessary. We'll keep you posted."

"Good luck, Aristotle," Ben called.

"Thank you. I wish you good luck also," the robot replied.

Ben had managed to get the engine of the berserker turned on. The same high-pitched whine they had heard earlier filled the air.

"It's a good thing this was designed to be operated from up here as well as by remote control," Ben said. "Since we knocked out most of the sensors, it would have been difficult to move it otherwise."

"Maowrr!" came a sound behind the boys.

"It's General Grant again," Tom exclaimed.

"The motor's vibrations must have disturbed his sleep." Ben said.

"Which way?" Tom asked Ahn.

The young alien pointed to the left.

Ben entered the instructions into the computer on the control panel.

"That's how this thing is steered?" Tom asked. "It seems much more complicated to enter a code into a computer than to simply push a lever or turn a wheel."

"Maybe they had a reason for doing it this way. Or maybe the other robots modified this control panel after they took over," Ben suggested. "Besides, I've never driven a ten-ton berserker through a jungle by entering codes into a computer," he grinned.

"There's a first for everything, I suppose," Tom answered. "Just make sure you don't push the wrong buttons. We don't want this baby to start tearing up trees again. No reason to leave more of a trail for the pursuing robots than we have to."

Not long afterward, they came to the edge of a clearing which was filled with robots. Some of them were covered with rust and ready to fall apart. Others looked almost brand-new. They were of every shape. Some had saws attached. Others were like the berserker in which the young people were riding. Still others had hoses sprouting from their bodies.

"Well, would you look at that!" Tom said.

"There's an entire army of them!" Ben exclaimed.

"Exactly!" Tom replied.

"Uh-oh! I don't like it when you get that sound in your voice!" Ben wailed in mock despair.

"Oh, you'll love this," Tom said. "I'm about to make you a general."

"*Maowrr!*" the black and brown cat protested. It jumped up from the floor onto the control panel and haughtily marched over to Tom, where it stared directly into the young inventor's face, its eyes never blinking. *"Maowrr!"* it growled again.

All three boys laughed.

"Okay, okay. You can be a general, too!" Tom promised the ruffled cat.

Satisfied, General Grant sat down on a narrow flat surface on the control panel and began to wash his head by licking his paws and rubbing them over his fur.

Ben grew serious again. "So I'm a general in the Swift Enterprises Army. Where are my troops?"

Tom pointed out the narrow windows in front of them. "Right there."

At the look on his friend's face, the young inventor added with a smile, "And you're going to lead them against the robots in the city!"

Chapter Fourteen

Before Ben could say anything, Tom explained his plan.

"Our most important job is to rescue Anita and Aristotle and to defeat the robots, right?"

When Ben nodded his agreement, Tom continued. "The only way to defeat them is by turning off the Unimind. But that must be done very carefully. We can't simply blow it up or pull its plug—assuming it's plugged into some power source and isn't self-sufficient."

"Why not?" asked Ahn.

"Because the Unimind obviously controls the entire city," Tom explained. "The lights, the 137 sewers, everything is run by it. So what we have to do is give it some knockout drops."

"What?" asked Ben.

"If the Unimind were a human being, we would not want to keep it from breathing, or stop its heart from beating, or any of its internal organs from functioning. All we'd want to do is to put it to sleep," Tom explained.

"We'd want to knock it out for the count," Ben exclaimed, suddenly understanding Tom's plan.

The young inventor nodded. "Exactly."

"And how do you propose to do that?" Ben asked.

"I'm going to build an electronic stunner. A device that will only knock out the part of the Unimind which is waging the anti–biological life campaign," Tom said.

"How are you going to do that?" Ben wanted to know.

"By sneaking back to the city and working with Aristotle," Tom replied calmly.

"Oh, no, you don't!" Ben shouted. "That would be *most* unhealthy for you. And, besides, you're not going anywhere without me!" Ben shook his head vigorously.

"Thanks for the sentiment, pal. But I've made up my mind," Tom said. "One of us has a better chance of sneaking into the city undiscovered than two. Your job will be to provide a diversion when the critical time comes."

At Ben's blank look, Tom explained further. "We're going to reprogram these deactivated machines—at least some of them. When I give the signal, you and some volunteers from the village will begin to harass the robots. Nothing too serious. We don't want anyone to be hurt. Just enough to get and keep their attention," he added.

Tom's face grew thoughtful. "That's when I'll attack the Unimind with the stunner. It won't be expecting a second attack. At least, it won't if we're lucky and manage to keep my presence in the city a secret."

"That's all pretty risky," Ben said dubiously.

"True," Tom admitted. "But considering the situation, I think that plan has the best chance of working." He looked out the window at the stilled robots.

"If we had a little more time—say, a couple of days—we could reprogram these robots to gradually take over the city. They could overpower the other robots one at a time or infiltrate the city's key areas and shut them down. But that would take too long."

Ben nodded. "Anita is in too much immediate danger for us to wait a couple of days."

The young Indian put a hand on Tom's shoulder. "I just hate the thought of abandoning you while you walk right into the lion's den, as the old saying goes."

Tom grinned at his friend. "You're not abandoning me. You're drawing the enemy's fire while I sneak behind their lines."

"And how do you propose to get behind the enemy lines?" Ahn asked.

"I'll go back to Mataste and the other cyborgs. They can sneak me into the city. Probably right into the building where Aristotle is. They know the sewers and the city's layout better than anyone else. A saboteur could hardly ask for better guides."

"Okay, you win," Ben replied. "Let's go inspect the troops."

The three boys and General Grant climbed out of the berserker and walked through the field to the abandoned robots.

"Notice anything unusual about them?" Tom asked Ben after a few minutes.

"I was just about to ask you the same question," Ben answered. "All the ones in good condition seem to be of the same metal—the metal of the berserker."

"My thought exactly," Tom said. "They were probably made from the metal of the spaceship that originally brought Ahn's ancestors here."

"Which would mean they were built about the same time. So they are all probably controlled the same way, as well," Ben pointed out.

Tom nodded. "That would make our job easier."

"If I could just hook them up to the same computer . . ." Ben's voice trailed off.

"What about the computer in the village?" Tom asked. "Maybe you could use it to boost the power of the computer in the berserker."

"That's possible," Ben agreed.

The trio climbed into the unrusted robots and examined their control panels carefully.

"They all seem to be in working order," Ben said in wonder. "So the thing for us to do is to go back to the village and get the computer and those plastic cards. We can hook it up to our berserker's computer and proceed from there."

" 'Our' berserker?" Tom asked with a grin.

"Well, yes. After all, we've spent so much time in and around it, I'm beginning to think of it as home," Ben admitted.

"*Maowrr!*" General Grant growled.

Tom laughed. "The cat sounds jealous! How far is it back to the village?" he asked Ahn.

"Only a little way," the alien replied. "We moved in its general direction when we drove the berserker here. Perhaps we should leave the robot here as camouflage?"

"Good idea. There's nothing more we can do here until we examine the computer in the village."

As the boys walked back through the jungle, Tom's head whirled with plans and alternate plans. He knew what they were about to do was risky. But he could not think of anything that promised results in such a short time.

Time! he thought. That's what we simply have too little of!

Part of his brain registered the jungle as they passed through it. The immense trees with their huge, brilliantly colored flowers Tom had noticed earlier. Now he noticed that their bigness was offset by incredibly small things all around them.

There were thousands of flowers as tiny as the nail of Tom's little finger. The butterflies were not much bigger than the common housefly on Earth. In fact, they looked like flies dressed for a masquerade party. The thought of hundreds of costumed houseflies going to a party made the young inventor laugh out loud.

"What's so funny?" Ben asked, puzzled by his friend's sudden gaiety.

When Tom explained about the houseflies and their party, Ben grinned. "I was noticing all the strange insects, too."

"And look at the tiny berries. And those mushrooms with the purple and orange spots." Tom shook his head. "It's so much like Earth in some ways and so totally different in others."

"Yes. This heavy gravity, for one thing!" Ben complained. "I manage to forget it for a while. But it always catches up with me!"

"I wonder what the core of the planet could be made out of to account for the heavier gravity," Tom said. "And for a planet so much like Earth, I wonder why human-type life never developed here."

"That's right," Ben added. "Ahn's ancestors arrived here to colonize it. They weren't natives of this place. I wonder if they knew about it or discovered it by accident."

"And where did they come from in the first place?" Tom mused. "There are so many similarities between them and us that there must be some connecting link."

"Maybe the computer in the village, or the Unimind, will be able to shed some light on the subject," Ben said.

As they walked past a green spider sitting in a pool of water in the folds of a giant leaf, Tom reluctantly closed his mind to the exotic life surrounding him. Right now they had something much more urgent to do.

When they reached the village, Tom and Ben headed for Teo's gourd-hut.

"I will explain your plan to my friends," Ahn said. "The volunteers and I will meet you at Teo's."

"Remember," Tom cautioned, "it will mean returning to the field you said was forbidden to your people. And the volunteers will have to spend time in and around the robots."

"It's also quite likely some of them'll be hurt when the going gets rough," Ben added.

"I will explain all of that," the alien said. "But I will also stress that this is our only hope against the robots and their plan to get rid of us all. For generations we have run from them, hiding any place we could. We have been unable to ever fight back."

Ahn's face reflected his inner defiance. "Finally, we have a chance to regain our pride and our city. We must do everything we can to aid you! I will tell them that, too! If we fail now, we will fail forever!"

Tom knew how much was at stake, how many people were counting on his plan, and he was moved by the trust the alien put in him. "Good luck," the young inventor said simply as he shook Ahn's hand.

"We'll be waiting at Teo's," Ben promised.

When the boys approached the older man's home, he greeted them warmly.

"What news do you have?" he asked anxiously.

When Tom and Ben explained how the remote-control device had caused the helicopter robot to crash, Teo's face broke into a smile.

"We have very little time," Tom said. "Aristotle thinks the computer and the plastic cards go together. May we run some experiments on them?"

"Of course, of course! Come with me," Teo said as he walked into his gourd-hut. He gestured to the black plastic box that stood on a table. "Please. Do whatever you need to do."

Eagerly, the boys went to work.

Ben pointed as Tom carefully removed the computer from its box. "There's the slot for the cards. I recharged the solar batteries at the same time I recharged the batteries for the remote-control device. It should be ready to go."

He looked at it for a moment. "How do you turn it on?" he asked Tom.

Both boys searched all over for a switch of some kind. But there was nothing but the keyboard on the computer's front.

Ben pushed the buttons, one by one. Nothing happened. His face fell.

"Maybe this will do it," Tom said, reaching for one of the plastic cards and inserting it into the slot.

Instantly, the computer began to hum!

"That's it!" Ben cried.

"Well, it *is* working," Tom admitted. "But I can't make heads or tails out of what's on the screen!"

"Teo," Ben called. "Can you help us, please? This card seems to be all words," he added, flipping through the program.

"Diagrams or mathematical formulas we would have a chance of deciphering. But an alien language is something else again," Tom said.

Eagerly, the elderly man peered at the lit computer screen.

"It is a history of our people," he said excitedly. "This is one of the Old Stories. It is about the Old Ones before they came to Ourworld."

Ben pulled the plastic card out of the computer and flipped it around. Again, the screen was filled with words.

Teo struggled through some of it before answering. "This one is much more difficult to understand. It seems to be about the early days the Old Ones spent on this planet. There is disagreement about building giant machines to clear the land."

The man's voice was full of emotion. He turned his eyes from the computer screen to the boys. "Do you realize what this means for us? We will no longer be a group of people in ignorance of our past. We will have a history! We will know who we are!"

Tom put his hand gently on Teo's shoulder. "I am happy for you. If we had more time I would be as anxious as you are to learn about your past. But right now we have to find out all we can about the Unimind and the robots, especially the communication system between the two."

"I understand," Teo said.

They examined several of the cards without success. None of them seemed to even come close to supplying the information the boys needed so desperately.

"Any other time my mouth would be drooling at all this," Ben said ruefully.

"I know," Tom agreed. "Detailed analysis of this planet, as well as several others nearby, descriptions of a star going supernova! My father would love to get his hands on that one! Plus all the history of Ourworld and wherever it was the Karshe lived before arriving here. This'll keep

Swift Enterprises' scientists and historians busy for years and years!"

"That's assuming we get the information back to them," Ben said. "Anyway, what we're looking for just isn't here."

"If it's not, then we'll have to muddle through without it," Tom said. "Let's try the last card."

The young inventor slipped the plastic card into the back of the computer. The screen lit up and all three of them crowded around, anxious to see what wonders it contained.

Both Tom and Ben held their breath. It was a diagram, a vaguely familiar-looking diagram!

"It looks like a computer's circuits that have gone haywire," Ben commented.

"What does it say at the bottom?" Tom asked Teo, pointing to the title of the diagram.

"It says this is something called the 'Central Connecting Circuitry for Projected Master Computer Terminal,'" Teo read hesitantly, stumbling over several of the words. "What does that mean?"

Tom and Ben threw their fists into the air and jumped up and down. "Hurrah! That's it! THAT'S IT!" Tom exclaimed.

Teo looked at the young inventor, puzzled. "It?" he asked.

"That's the Unimind!" Tom cried.

Chapter Fifteen

It was clear to the boys that there was far more information available to them than they would ever be able to read, never mind use for their upcoming battle.

"Just sort out a couple of things," Tom said. "We need to know where the major components of the Unimind are. Where are the sections dealing with the routine running of the city?"

Ben pointed to one side of the diagram. "It seems sections A-1179 through D-4278 deal with routine functions. I'm not sure which of those are running the city and which are concerned with other things," he said. "Those circuits are fairly simple and are set up to run continuously. 149

Only in the event of a malfunction would they even notify the main part of the computer."

"Is there any way to tell which section of the computer is responsible for *taking over* the city and for the war against us?" Tom asked.

"I can only guess, but it's probably this part," Ben said. "See, the circuitry is very complex and capable of complicated changes. Most of the rest simply is dealing with storage of information. It serves as a buffer zone between the two parts of the computer."

"So if the stunner is too strong, it might knock out some of the storage circuits before damaging the vital-functions area?" Tom asked.

Ben nodded. "That's how it looks, according to this. But don't forget, this diagram is very old. The Unimind has been in control of things for generations. It might have evolved into something quite different from the way it appears here," he warned.

Tom shook his head. "I don't think so. Remember, Aristotle said the robots were all very simple? I don't believe the robots—or the Unimind—are able to evolve into anything more complex than what they were when the humanoids first built them."

Ben pointed to an area of complex circuitry on the screen. "But think of all the different robots we saw in the city. Who knows what they might have come up with over the last few decades?"

"But none of the ones we saw were very complex," Tom objected. "Lots of robots, yes. In fact, a different one for each task. No single robot seemed to do more than one thing. That argues for the Unimind not being able to advance beyond what it was at its conception."

Ben thought for a minute. "You have a point there," he admitted. "I hope you're right, ol' buddy."

"So do I!" Tom grinned.

The young inventor explained to Teo what they planned to do. When the old man learned that Tom planned to go back into the sewers and work with the cyborgs, he looked around the room, as if making sure they were alone.

"Ahn told you our people are very afraid of the cyborgs. The least hint that a person had been near them or in the sewers is enough to cut that person off from the village forever!" he warned.

"Yet Ahn knows the sewers and the cyborgs," Tom commented.

"Ahn is very much like his father was," Teo said. "His father, too, was impatient at our ignorance. He was convinced the things from the Old Ones held the keys to our triumphing over the

Metal Ones." The old man's eyes got a faraway look in them, as if he were seeing events that had happened years before.

"Ahn's father made several trips into the city. He was looking for something which would unlock the secrets he was sure the black box contained. He uncovered much information about the Metal Ones. He also convinced the villagers that regular spying trips should be made into the city to gather information. But he was never able to get the answers he wanted about the black box."

The old man's face filled with sorrow. "He was a great leader! When the robots captured him, it was indeed a black day for our village."

"And he was never seen again?" Ben asked softly.

"No. There are rumors that Ahn's father has been made a cyborg."

Tom and Ben gasped. "Does Ahn know this?" Tom asked.

"Yes. He has tried to find his father in the sewer, but had no success."

No wonder Ahn was not afraid of the cyborgs, Tom thought, and had made friends with them. He recalled how helpful Mataste had been to the humans because they were with Ahn, and the pain the giant had felt at being shunted by his people.

"I think I'll be in very good hands with Ma-taste," Tom said. "He and his friends will help us."

The sounds of approaching footsteps reached them, putting an end to the conversation.

The boys hurried out of the gourd-hut to see Ahn and a couple dozen of the villagers walking their way.

"We are ready," Ahn said. "Tell us what you want us to do."

"First of all, we have to take the computer back to the berserker. Then Ben and I will have several hours of work to do," Tom said.

"We will take you back to the berserker and wait for you there," Ahn said, and the others nodded.

Teo disappeared inside his home. When he came back, he handed the two boys the black plastic box with the computer and the cards.

"I will not see you again until after you battle with the Metal Ones. My thoughts go with you," he said.

"Thank you," Tom said sincerely.

"We'll see you soon," Ben called as the group began to move into the jungle.

Several hours later, the work was as ready as it could be.

The computer was installed in the original berserker and linked with three other robots.

While Ben was working on the communications network, Tom salvaged equipment from the robots and made two radios. They were very simple and would work only for short distances, but they would have to do.

"Well, I suppose this is it," Tom said to Ben. "Give me a hard copy of the circuits for the Unimind. It's possible Aristotle hasn't been allowed access to that information yet."

While Ben ran off the data, Tom surveyed the scene.

"What an army," the young inventor said. "Two Terrans, twenty-three humanoids, four slightly recycled robots . . ."

"And one cat," Ben said, grinning, and pointed to General Grant, who had appeared out of nowhere and was rubbing his head against Tom's legs.

Tom smiled at Ben. "You like this, don't you?"

Ben shrugged. "Well, it's not every day a computer technician is asked to reprogram four giant alien robots and head into battle without sleeping. I admit I'm curious about what will happen. By the way, we haven't named these things yet. Do you have any ideas?"

"What about Berserkers Number One, Two, Three, and Four?" Tom asked.

"You sometimes display a frightening lack of creative imagination," Ben complained.

"Me? Lacking in imagination?" Tom exclaimed.

"I said *sometimes*," Ben defended himself.

Tom turned to Ahn and his friends, and told them his strategy. "We're going toward the city," he concluded. "You all know where you belong and have been given a specific job to do. We will move very slowly so you can get used to the berserkers. After I leave, Ben will put you through some practice maneuvers."

He grinned impishly at his friend. "Okay," he shouted. "Head 'em up—move 'em out!"

Ben laughed. "I know where you got that from. I took a class in historical television, too!"

"And you said I have no creative imagination," Tom said.

"Isn't there going to be any stirring music?" Ben replied. "No bugle? Not even any bagpipes? Okay, okay—we can do without it," he muttered as Tom reached for his throat.

As they settled themselves at the control panel, Ben lifted the mike to his lips. "Everyone ready?" he called into it.

Ahn, who was in charge of one of the berserkers, answered, "Ready here." The other two were also ready.

"Let's go!" Ben called.

The screech of metal long left without proper maintenance filled the air. Brush crackled underfoot as the robots started off.

Ahn and the other two pilots adapted quickly to communicating with microphones and carrying out Ben's instructions.

The young computer tech was all smiles. "You would think these guys were part Indian," he said to Tom. "It's hard to believe a few hours ago they didn't know what a radio or a remote-control switch was."

Tom nodded. "You're a good teacher. Now remember, wait until you get the signal from me before you do anything except practice a few maneuvers. That's going to be hard, I know. Stay hidden in the jungle until I locate Aristotle and we get the stunner put together."

"Why don't you call him on the radio, outline our plan, and give him some guidelines?" Ben asked. "That way he'll be able to think about it and start working on the stunner."

"Good idea," Tom agreed. "I'll discuss the design with him during our trip to the city."

Several hours later, Ahn's voice came over the berserker's radio. "We're approaching our destination!"

"Stop forward motion," Ben ordered. The caravan drew to a halt about a mile from the edge of the jungle. Just beyond was the sewer entrance where Mataste had promised a cyborg would always be waiting.

"Okay, Ben, I'll see you when this is all over," Tom said as he got to his feet.

"Take care of yourself, buddy," Ben said, trying to hide the fear he felt.

The cat jumped down from the control panel where he had been sitting for the entire ride. He followed Tom out the door of the berserker.

"Looks like General Grant would rather take his chances with you than stay with us," Ben said into his radio.

"Well, cats are supposed to have nine lives. Maybe he wants to get rid of a few," Tom suggested.

Ben watched his friend walk quickly into the jungle. Tom turned back once more to the four berserkers and saluted. Then he disappeared from view.

He walked rapidly through the dense vegetation, his mind focused on what had to be done. About twenty minutes later he came within sight of the jungle's edge and stopped. He listened intently for the sounds of any robot helicopters, but heard nothing. Cautiously, he made his way to a huge tree. Shielded from sight, Tom watched for several minutes, but saw no robot patrols.

He spotted the camouflaged sewer entrance and took a deep breath. "Okay, General Grant, we take this at a run."

With that, he raced for the sewer.

Chapter Sixteen

Tom and his black and brown cat streaked across the open ground, disappearing into the sewer entrance.

At the bottom of the ladder, Tom suddenly came face to face with one of the two cyborgs who were guarding the entrance. Even though he was expecting it and knew what the cyborgs looked like, he was still momentarily shocked.

"Uh, I'm Tom Swift. Mataste said someone here would be able to take me to him," the young inventor said.

Without saying a word, the cyborg nodded twice, then walked down the dark tunnel at the back of the stairwell.

Tom hesitated for a moment, then decided he was supposed to follow.

After twisting and turning, the tunnel finally opened into the cavern where Tom and Ben had first talked with Mataste. Mataste was sitting at a crude table with three other cyborgs. When he saw Tom, he stood up and raised his hands in greeting.

"Tom! How good to see you!" His voice boomed throughout the cavern.

"Mataste, I need your help against the robots," Tom said.

"Certainly! I promised help," the cyborg replied. "What are your plans?"

Tom quickly outlined the course of action and told him that when the critical time arrived, Ben, Ahn, and the others would create a distraction.

"That is where we can help," Mataste said thoughtfully. "We have been making small troubles against the robots for some time now. Nothing too big, but enough to spot some of their weak points."

Tom pulled out his radio and called Ben. Mataste peered at it curiously, but otherwise showed no surprise. Several of the other cyborgs drew back in fright when Ben's voice sounded through the small speaker.

"Ben, I have help for you," Tom said. "Mataste

and the cyborgs will assist you in creating your distraction. He says they have discovered some weaknesses in the robots you will be able to take advantage of."

"Sounds like you're turning into quite a recruiting officer, Mister Swift," Ben joked. *"That's terrific news. Incidentally, Ahn and the others have taken to driving the berserkers as if they were born in them. We're itching for some action, so don't take too long down there. Over and out."*

Tom noticed that at Ben's praise of Ahn, Mataste smiled for a moment. Obviously, he was very fond of the young alien.

"Now we'll have to locate Aristotle," Tom said.

"I will go with you to find your robot," Mataste told him. He turned to two cyborgs next to him. "Gio and Krug, you round up the others—all who have been in raiding parties before. Take them to the two south entrances and begin infiltrating the jungle. Find Ben and Ahn about a mile into the jungle and wait for me there."

As the two cyborgs hurried off, he turned back to Tom. "This way," he said, heading for a tunnel straight in front of them.

They moved quickly through a number of passages and ducts. Fortunately, the water level was very low. Tom spotted a familiar landmark here and there. It was difficult for him to believe all that had happened since the last time he had walked through these tunnels!

"How do you plan to get to your friend?" Mataste asked.

"When we're in the main building, I'll radio him," Tom explained. "He will tell me where he is, and then this—," Tom held up the remote-control device, "—will help me deal with any robots I run into along the way."

Mataste stopped suddenly. "That is from the black box," he said with awe.

Tom briefly explained how they had used the device to bring down the spy helicopter. He also told how the computer and the plastic cards were helping to fight the robots.

"I knew it," Mataste said softly. "I knew those things would free us! This is indeed a happy day."

A few minutes later, he pointed to the end of a tunnel. "That is the stairwell you descended before," he said.

Tom found Aristotle's frequency on his radio and switched the power on.

"Tom, where are you?" Aristotle asked.

"In the sewer underneath the building where you found us the last time. Are you still in that building?" he asked.

"Yes. On the second floor. I am being asked to

implant advanced circuitry in the robots. I dislike doing the work, so I am going very slowly. However, I am afraid I have almost completed one of the robots. It will not be long before it—"

"Aristotle!" Tom cut him off. "What about Anita?"

"Oh, I am sorry. Here I go chattering on about my problems which are, of course, nothing compared with hers. She is fighting the reprograming, but her resistance is wearing down rapidly," the mechanoid said. *"There is quite a bit more to the library than I originally thought. It seems there are vast areas—,"* he began again before Tom cut him off.

"I'm signing off. I'll be with you in a few minutes," the young inventor said. Then he clicked off the radio before Aristotle could reply.

He turned to Mataste. "Thank you for your help. I know Ben joins me in welcoming you. Your aid will be as appreciated this time as it was before," he added, thinking about the last time Mataste had come to his rescue.

Mataste smiled briefly, then raised one hand in salute before walking back down the tunnel.

Tom climbed the stairs as quickly as he could. When he came to the wall at the top, he pressed his ear against it. He could not hear anything. But that might be because the wall was so thick it would be impossible to eavesdrop.

"Only one way to find out," Tom muttered. He pulled the small disk Aristotle had given him out of his pocket, and placed it on the wall. A door slid open!

Tom immediately flattened himself against the wall on the sewer side. When no robots appeared, he cautiously peered around the corner.

The hall was empty.

He reached behind him for the disk, then ran on tiptoe to a flight of stairs that he had spied in the distance. Racing up, he was just congratulating himself on his good fortune when he heard a noise.

It was the unmistakable tread of heavy metal feet!

Tom looked around. There was no place to hide!

He took out the remote-control device, but planned to use it only as a last resort. Using it inside the building was far too likely to alert the Unimind that something was wrong.

The young inventor flattened himself against the corner wall. If he was lucky, the robot would simply walk past without spotting him. That is, if he was lucky.

The steps grew closer and Tom instinctively held his breath.

A squat robot lumbered past the wall, stopped, and peered directly at the young man!

"There you are. I was hoping to find you."

"Aristotle!" Tom hissed. "Thank heavens it's you!"

"This way. Quickly!" the robot said as he began to retrace his steps toward an open door.

Suddenly, General Grant streaked past them, raced down the hall, and darted through the open door. Tom decided it was futile to attempt to keep up with the cat.

The laboratory was clean and cool. It looked much like other electronics facilities Tom had seen, except the workbenches were at three different heights. A partially disassembled robot lay on a bench near Tom's knees. The young man decided that must be the robot Aristotle had almost rewired.

"Where's Anita?" Tom asked anxiously. "We've got to rescue her and then get to the Unimind."

"Anita's signal has stopped entirely," Aristotle said. "Its cessation was abrupt. I am afraid they have captured her mind. It is all my fault."

"Can she be saved?" Tom asked quickly.

"Of course. Any programing can be erased," the robot replied. "But if we found her now, she would be one of the enemy. Our only hope is in defeating the Unimind first. Then we can help Anita."

When he saw the look on Tom's face, Aristotle put one metal hand on the young man's shoulder. "Truly, I am sorry, Tom. I know your code insists on rescuing Anita first. But, believe me, by concentrating on the Unimind, you are rescuing Anita."

The young inventor nodded. "I know you're right, Aristotle."

He showed Aristotle the copy of the Unimind circuits. "Does this look familiar?" he asked. "We found it in an old computer program."

Aristotle studied the hard copy and then shook his head. "There is one entire section of the library which is off-limits to all robots. I have tried to gain access in several different ways, but the security is too tight. Undoubtedly, that is the Unimind's property."

He studied the printout further. "This looks just as I thought it might. Of course, you understand I am making that assumption based only on my limited observation and—"

"You are a flawed mechanism," Tom finished with a grin.

"How did you know I was going to say that, Tom?" Aristotle asked.

"I built you, remember?" Tom replied. He

looked around the lab. "Are you sure this place is a safe place for us to work? I'd hate to finish this project only to discover the Unimind had been watching us all the time."

"The Unimind has no need for spy cameras or microphones," Aristotle reminded Tom. "Wherever any of its robots are, the Unimind is also. I am constantly sending relevant data back to it. As long as I do that, we are safe."

"Data?" Tom asked.

"The information I am sending indicates I am quite busily building a circuit board to bypass a major technical flaw in this robot," Aristotle said, indicating the mechanoid on the workbench.

"Okay." Tom selected a section of workbench and cleared it off. He handed Aristotle a scribe.

"Scratch the diagram for the stunner here and I'll see if I can improve it."

Aristotle's metal hand cut the design into the tabletop quickly, then Tom bent over it.

"Hmm. Simple induction coil," he mused, "but quite powerful and efficient. I don't suppose there was anything in the library about a Unimind-sized stunner?"

The squat mechanoid shook his head. "You want me to beef this up a bit?"

"I think it would be safer."

Twenty minutes later, Tom looked at the improved design. "Not bad," he said aloud. "See if you can find any flaws."

The robot scanned the diagram in a second. "In terms of efficiency, it is an improvement," he admitted. "However, it is somewhat larger than the original sketch."

"It's a rush job," Tom said. "You can't have everything."

Tom and Aristotle had just finished assembling the instrument from the materials readily available in the electronics lab, when a sound came from beneath the table.

"Maowrr?"

"Oh, hi, cat," Tom said as General Grant's tail wound around his legs. Absently, he bent down to scratch its neck.

At that instant, something hit the top of the table with great force! A shower of equipment filled the laboratory. The cat disappeared.

Tom ducked and saw the supposedly inactive robot moving. It rose like a vampire in a horror movie, its body in parts, supported by one arm.

The half-assembled creature struck out again. Using a bar of metal which had been leaning against the bench, it ripped a chunk from the edge of the plastic table.

Tom rolled, cutting himself on the wreckage strewn on the floor. He kicked at the robot as it struck at him again. The bar made a hole in the floor next to Tom's head!

Tom kicked once more, but his blow simply bounced off the heavy mechanoid.

Now the robot seized Tom's leg and tugged. The arm with the bar flailed in the air and prepared to crash down yet another time. There was no way Tom could avoid the blow!

Suddenly, something flashed before Tom's eyes. It was the charging body of Aristotle!

The bulky robot smashed a metal forearm into the descending bar, and the crash of steel rang thoughout the lab.

The Unimind robot released its grip on Tom's ankle and the young man jerked free.

Aristotle delivered a powerful blow straight to the chest of the attacker, crunching through its body and crushing the computerbrain within.

The enemy robot stopped moving. Its arm dropped and the steel bar fell to the floor with a clang before rolling against the wall.

There was silence.

"Thanks, Aristotle. You've done it again," Tom said gratefully.

"*Maowrr?*" General Grant said, nosing Tom's ear.

Tom reached for the cat. "And you, too. I owe both of you my life. You, General, for making me bend over when I did. And you, Aristotle, for tackling that robot at just the right time."

"You gave me life, Tom. Even if I am a flawed mechanism, I am proud to have helped you," Aristotle declared.

"Proud?" Tom asked. "Emotion, old friend?"

"Of course. You programed me for satisfaction in achievement, in excellence, and in quality of my work. Is that not pride? Have I misinterpreted something subtly human?" he asked.

Tom smiled. "No, Aristotle. You have it right." He put General Grant on the floor and got to his feet. Suddenly, he realized the immediate danger they were in.

"Aristotle—that robot would not have acted in such a hostile fashion if it were not still controlled by the Unimind!"

"That is correct," Aristotle replied. "The Unimind will be aware of its malfunction."

"Which means we'll have to hurry. Some robot is bound to arrive soon to check on its buddy. Do we have a self-contained power pack?"

"Inventory for this section indicated two suitable batteries," Aristotle replied. "I have taken the liberty of getting one out to be used on the stunner. I hope that was not incorrect of me?"

"Not at all. Let's put it in. Now, are we ready?"

"I can think of nothing else unless you want to test it first," the mechanoid suggested.

"No time for that. We have to get out of here," Tom said. He pulled out his radio and called Ben.

"Ben? It's time for a little diversion out there. Are Mataste and the cyborgs there yet?" he asked.

"They're here and full of good ideas. This is going to be fun!" Ben enthused.

"Just don't get so carried away you forget the robots are deadly. They've got that chemical which they might try on you guys!" Tom cautioned.

"Don't worry, good buddy. None of us are about to give them a chance!" Ben said. *"We're ready any time."*

"Then start NOW!" Tom called. He clicked off his radio and turned to Aristotle. "Show me where the Unimind is!" he said.

Chapter Seventeen

Aristotle led Tom out of the building and, via the sewer, into another city square. They exited in front of a hemisphere of glistening metal. The sun glinted off the polished surface with almost painful brilliance.

"Is that it?" Tom asked.

Aristotle nodded.

"How do we get in?"

"The entrance is there." The robot pointed. "That disk of metal. It's the floor of an elevator."

Tom stopped, hefting the stunner in his hand. "Is that the only entrance? I would hate to be at the mercy of whoever is at the other end of the elevator. We'd be trapped. Which is probably why they built it that way," he added.

"Checking city construction plans, Tom," Aristotle said. He used his radio link with the library computer. "There is a bricked-up entrance on the lower level of that building," he said, pointing to a cone-shaped structure a few feet away.

Tom started to run. As they entered the structure, two bright-blue robots came at them. One brandished a brightly polished steel bar.

Before Tom could say anything, Aristotle moved forward, putting himself between Tom and the two threatening robots. He used a karate move to block the blow of the bar. Then he threw the attacking robot head first against a sloping wall!

The second robot started to charge past, but Aristotle used a sidekick to punch through the attacker's chest and stop it permanently.

"You—," Tom stuttered in utter surprise. "Where did you ever learn something like that?"

"I read a lot, Tom. You will find a vast number of interesting bits of information in books."

Tom chuckled. Aristotle never ceased to amaze him. "Where's the entrance?" he asked.

"Down below. Follow me."

They went to the lowest level of the complex.

There, amid the pipes and wires, they found the sealed door. Aristotle's metal muscles quickly punched a hole through it and they found themselves in a dark passage.

"It will probably interest you to know that Ben and his troops are causing the robots quite a bit of trouble," Aristotle whispered as they picked their way forward. "I cannot understand exactly what is going on since I am monitoring the robots' reports to the Unimind. They seem very confused."

Tom grinned in the darkness. Good ol' Ben, he thought. You could always trust him to come through at the crucial moment!

They finally came to a cavernous room which seemed to have no ceiling. Before Tom could ask any questions, there was a resounding crash!

"STOP!"

The voice thundered through the room.

"This way, Tom," Aristotle said, running to the left.

The chamber was brightly lit and spherical. Except for a few feet of clearance around the exterior, and some maintenance passageways through it, the gigantic computer which was the Unimind filled the hundred-foot-diameter cavern. Its size was nothing short of awesome.

"STOP!" cried the voice again.

Tom ignored it, only to have a bolt of laser fire burst through the room. The ruby-red flame narrowly missed the young inventor, just singeing the shoulder of his jumpsuit.

Before the laser could fire again, Aristotle rammed the pole the laser gun stood on, sending it crashing to the floor.

Tom followed Aristotle to the very heart of the spherical brain. There he fixed the stunner firmly to the circuits.

"Stop!" It was a different voice and Tom whirled to see where it came from. A figure in fiery red was running toward him.

It was Anita Thorwald in clothes so fantastic Tom could only think of them as a costume. Bright-red armor, a winged helmet of the same color, and mailed gloves made up the outfit. She carried a bright bar of steel which Tom thought must be the standard weapon of the robots.

Anita charged at Tom with glaring eyes, a piercing scream coming from her throat!

"Anita!" Tom cried. "Anita! It's me—Tom Swift. I'm your friend!"

"I know who you are, you puny creature!" she shouted. "How dare you defy the Unimind!"

Tom noticed Anita's leg. Her metallic-cloth

jumper had been neatly cut away, and a device about the size of a fist had been attached to her computer.

The young man looked into Anita's eyes. "We've come to take you home," he said desperately.

Anita glanced at Aristotle.

"We're your friends," Tom pleaded.

"My *friends*!" Anita spat bitterly. "No such luck, Swift! You had me fooled for a while, but not anymore! I have my head in shape now. I know you for what you are!"

She advanced slowly but threateningly. "Get out of here, Swift! Nobody wants you here, you . . . you *human*!"

"Anita, you're human, too!"

"Not anymore!" Anita's eyes blazed. "Once I was weak, but now I have gone beyond that! I shall soon become even stronger!"

She lifted the metal bar over her head effortlessly. "They improved me! They . . ." Her voice faltered.

As Tom stared in amazement, Anita's personality suddenly seemed to change. She crouched, her hands close to her body. The arrogant anger left her face and she pleaded, "Get away, Tom. Quickly. The railing, it's . . ." Her voice choked off abruptly.

"Anita, what's wrong?" Tom asked. "Here, let me help you," he pleaded, moving toward her.

"Run . . . before   they   change . . . you . . . into . . ."

Then her back straightened and her eyes blazed once again. "Into something you are not, Swift! You're human. Vermin! How dare you come here! You will pay!"

She raised the metal bar again.

Tom could not take the chance of her weapon smashing the stunner. He knew he could not count on Aristotle to help him. The robot's programing was quite specific about not harming human beings in any way. As far as Aristotle was concerned, Anita, though under the control of the Unimind, was still a human being.

Anita swirled the metal bar over her head. Tom waited until the very last moment, then dived right for her feet. She struck at him with the bar, but she was off-balance and missed. She crashed onto the maintenance way. Tom rolled to his feet.

Anita stood up and advanced more slowly this time, but still with deadly determination. Except for her face, she was completely covered with metal. The linkage and flexibility of the tiny plates were flawless, and the crash had not dented her armor in the slightest.

Tom bit his lower lip. His friend looked as if she had evolved from some sort of shiny beetle!

Anita leaped at him again, swinging the gleaming bar down in a vicious attack. Tom flew across the walkway, then jumped onto her back.

Get to her carotid artery, he said to himself desperately. Cut off the supply of blood to her brain. She'll go unconscious in a few seconds, but won't be in any danger.

But the new Anita was too strong for him. She bucked once and sent him flying over her head. He crashed on the walkway with stunning force. But he rolled over instantly. Anita's steel bar ripped through the heavy mesh of the walk where he had been only a split-second before!

Tom yelled, "Activate the stunner, Aristotle!"

He scrambled to his feet and raced away from the robot, hoping to draw Anita with him so that Aristotle would not be endangered.

Anita slipped and fell. Her foot caught in the walkway. She looked at Tom with a new look in her eye. "Oh, Tooommm. I . . . I . . . can't . . . help . . ."

"You can't control it. I know. Just hold on one more minute! That's all I need. One minute!" He looked over his shoulder. "Aristotle! *Activate the stunner!*"

There was no response!

Tom saw that Anita was hunched over, sweating. Her whole body was trembling. He turned and ran for the heart of the complex that was the Unimind.

He rounded the corner and saw that Aristotle was motionless, one hand on the railing, the other reaching for the controls of the stunner.

The railing!

The Unimind had electrified the railing and burned Aristotle out!

Aristotle was dead!

Tom knew that if he touched the stunner he would be just as dead as Aristotle.

His sneakers! Of course!

He poised on one foot and used the toe of one sneaker to close the switch for the first phase. Then he heard feet pounding on the walkway behind him.

Ignore that, he said to himself.

Sequence two.

Sequence two activated.

The sequence-three switch was too small for the toe of his sneaker. What could he use?

Feet continued to pound down the walkway.

Tom knew he had only seconds left. This was his very last chance!

He unfastened the straps to his jumpsuit and pulled his knit cotton sportshirt over his head. Folding it several times to make a hotpad, the young inventor reached out and threw the third and final switch.

The stunner activated.

An enormous roar filled the cavernous chamber and all the lights went out. Then Anita screamed!

Chapter Eighteen

A few minutes later, the dusty, sweaty forms of Tom Swift and Anita Thorwald came out from the depths of the building into the sunlight.

Anita had lost her helmet, but her sleek red armor was still on. Tom's shirt had an enormous tear in it, but otherwise he was fine.

They stopped and took deep breaths.

Tom flipped on his radio. "Ben? Ben? Are you there?" he called anxiously.

"What did you do, Tom?" came Ben's cheerful voice from the speaker. *"Everything was going fine and suddenly the cowboys just stopped still. They're all standing absolutely frozen, as if someone just pulled the plug from them!"*

"Since the Unimind's circuits that control the robots were turned off, I suppose you might say someone pulled the plug," Tom agreed.

"I might have known something like that would happen," Ben complained.

"What on earth are you talking about?" Anita asked.

"Hi, Anita. We were just playing a little game of Cowboys and Indians here. Ahn and the others are terrific Indians, I must say. Of course, we didn't have any bows and arrows," he added.

Tom and Anita heard a low chuckle from their friend. *"Funny, The berserkers thought that trees would make good arrows, so they started using them like that. Really did serious damage to the poor robots who were playing cowboys."*

He growled in mock anger. *"Trust you, Swift, to ruin the first chance I get to make the Indians win a serious game like this!"*

The two young people laughed.

"Any injuries, Ben?" Tom asked.

"A couple of scratches, that's all," Ben said.

"We'll meet you back at the *Exedra*," Tom called. "Over and out."

Anita bent over and depressed a section of the metal growth on her leg. It fell off with a clunk.

"That's better," she said. She kicked it aside.

"I think I'm going to build some kind of

one-way circuit into my leg so that kind of thing can't happen again," she said.

"I'll help you," Tom said. "But first we'd better get Aristotle to a lab!"

The young people went back into the building, which was now lit with emergency lights.

"If we push him together, we should be able to get him to the *Exedra*," Tom said.

When they half-dragged, half-shoved Aristotle to the *Exedra*, Tom and Anita found Ben sitting happily on top of one of the berserkers. A crowd of humanoids and cyborgs were scattered about.

Ben looked at Anita and his eyes grew wide. "What are you dressed up for—Amazon Week?"

Anita was embarrassed. "Well, I think this was the Unimind's idea of a female robot."

Ben spotted Aristotle and clambered down from the berserker. "What happened to him?"

Tom explained, and Ben helped his friends maneuver Aristotle into the spaceship's lab.

"General Grant, get down from there before you hurt yourself!" Tom called sternly.

The dirty brown and black cat was hopping onto equipment and over the tables in the lab. It completely ignored the young inventor and continued its random route until it reached the top of an electrical monitor.

"Maowrr!" it called down to the young inventor.

Aristotle remained silent and unmoving.

The three friends worked quickly for several minutes.

"We've got continuity!" said Ben excitedly. He stood up from the computer terminal and smiled at Tom. "There does not appear to be any leakage from the nuclear cell, either!"

Tom reached into the pocket of his jumpsuit and took out his ring of keys. On it, a small metal disk with uneven sides jangled. Tom put one edge of the disk into a slot of the same size on Aristotle's mainframe. A small drawer slid out silently.

All but one of the circuit boards appeared to be in good condition. Carefully, the young inventor lifted out something that had once been a circuit board.

Now it was nothing but a lump of black glass with a few metal streaks on it.

"Here's the problem," said Tom. "We need to replace his circuit."

"Good thing Aristotle and I are circuit brothers," Anita said. "Ever since the first accident in the lab, my computer has carried a memory of his circuits and he has a record of mine. You have all the information you need right here," she said, pointing to her leg.

It took several hours of intense work, but finally Tom had all of the intricate circuitry in place. Carefully, he replaced the circuit boards in the drawer and slid it shut.

Aristotle's eyes glowed and he looked at Tom.

"Something has happened," he said, and looked around the lab of the *Exedra*.

"If you ask, 'Where am I?' I think I'll twist one of your circuits around the wrong way." Ben laughed.

"I know very well where I am," Aristotle replied. "And since I have read many more books than you have, I am aware that almost never does one ask that question in real life. However, I confess I am a bit unsure of what happened before I got here."

Tom and his friends took turns filling the robot in on the events that took place during the last few hours. At the conclusion, the young inventor said, "Now let's go outside and talk to Ahn and his friends."

Noting Anita's puzzled look, Tom sighed. "There sure is a lot of storytelling to do here!"

"Never mind." The redhead laughed, hooking

her arm through Tom's. "I'm sure I'll figure it out soon enough. Come on!"

General Grant jumped down from the computer monitor and raced to the hatch where he preened for everyone.

"If you're not careful, that cat's going to own the *Exedra* before long!" Anita said.

"That'll be the day!" Tom shuddered.

Outside, they found Ahn, the villagers, and the cyborgs talking excitedly.

"Good news!" Ahn told the humans. "My friends have realized how wrong it was to shun the cyborgs. All those who wish to can return to our community. In fact," he added, "Mataste was unanimously asked to lead our people!"

Mataste grinned proudly. "We have a city to resettle and history to explore. We will need to find answers to many questions."

"And perhaps someday I will even find my father," Ahn said wistfully.

Mataste looked at him. "Now that we are no longer outcasts, I will tell you. I did not want you to be ashamed of me, Ahn. You see, I—I am Tor, your father."

Ahn's eyes filled with tears. He threw his arms around the giant cyborg. "I would never have been ashamed of you, never!" he said.

Mataste just smiled. Then he turned to Tom and his friends. "Will you stay with us, even for a few weeks? We need your talents desperately and you have many skills that have been lost to us for generations. Please stay for a while."

Tom looked at the others. "It would be a terrific opportunity for us to study a similiar but alien culture," he said.

"I, for one, can't wait to explore the things that have bothered me since we first got here," Ben spoke up.

"I'm game," said Anita. "After all, I haven't been allowed to see very much except the inside of a laboratory!"

"Though I am not a human and, therefore, not strictly entitled to a vote, I do think it would behoove us to answer some questions before beginning another adventure," Aristotle put in.

"Tom, what did you do to that replacement circuit?" Ben asked. " 'Behoove.' That's a new word for our robot."

"Another adventure?" Anita asked. "Don't tell me Aristotle is now gaining some of my empathic abilities!" She laughed.

Little did any of them know how right Aristotle was. Before too long, Tom and his friends would be entangled in *Tom Swift: Ark Two.*

"Everyone votes to stay, then?" Tom said.

"*Maowrr!*" growled General Grant from the ground.

He turned and walked with great dignity toward the center of the city, his tail high in the air, never once looking back.

Tom laughed. "*Now* I suppose everyone has voted!"